Championship Ball

BOOKS BY

CLAIR BEE

TECHNICAL

Basketball
Winning Basketball Plays
The Basketball Coach's Handbook
The Clair Bee Basketball Quiz Book
Basketball for Future All-American Stars
Basketball for Everyone
Make the Team in Basketball

The CLAIR BEE *Basketball Library*

The Science of Coaching
Basketball Fundamentals and Techniques
Individual and Team Basketball Drills
Man-to-Man Defense and Attack
Zone Defense and Attack

FICTION

The CHIP HILTON *Stories*

Touchdown Pass
Championship Ball
Strike Three!
Clutch Hitter!
Hoop Crazy
Pitchers' Duel
A Pass and a Prayer
Dugout Jinx
Freshman Quarterback
Backboard Fever
Fence Busters
Ten Seconds to Play!
Fourth Down Showdown
Tournament Crisis
Hardcourt Upset
Pay-Off Pitch
No-Hitter
Triple-Threat Trouble
Backcourt Ace
Buzzer Basket

As the ball arched high in the air, the timer's gun exploded

Championship Ball

A *CHIP HILTON* SPORTS STORY

Championship Ball

BY CLAIR BEE

GROSSET & DUNLAP Publishers New York

To

SY LOBELLO

Patriot, Student, Athlete

He gave all he had for his country

and his team

Sy Lobello was graduated from Long Island University in 1941 with a Bachelor of Science degree. While a student at the university, he played three years of varsity basketball and captained the team in 1940–41. He was killed in the Battle of the Bulge, December, 1944.

Contents

CHAPTER		PAGE
I	WHO'S A QUITTER?	1
II	SCRAPBOOK MEMORIES	14
III	A CHIP OFF THE OLD BLOCK	26
IV	THREE-MAN BASKETBALL	38
V	NICKNAMES WIN GAMES	46
VI	BASKETBALL CALISTHENICS	54
VII	PICKING THE VARSITY	64
VIII	THE YOUNG JOURNALIST	70
IX	WORDS FROM THE BENCH	77
X	REPETITION PAYS	83
XI	FIRST BLOOD	90
XII	THE ALUMNI GAME	98
XIII	FREEZE THE BALL	105
XIV	COACH ROCKWELL SPEAKS HIS MIND	118
XV	SHARPSHOOTERS	124
XVI	THE MISSING BOX	130

XVII	VF Takes to the Road	.	.	.	.	137
XVIII	The Harder They Fall	.	.	.	.	149
XIX	The Box Turns Up	.	.	.	.	158
XX	The Score That Counts	.	.	.	.	166
XXI	Down the Stretch	.	.	.	.	173
XXII	Dark Horse of the Tourney	.	.	.	183
XXIII	Locker Room Strategy	.	.	.	.	190
XXIV	Most Valuable Player	.	.	.	.	199
XXV	His Father's Son	.	.	.	.	205

Championship Ball

CHAPTER 1

WHO'S A QUITTER!

THE front wheels of the jalopy wobbled uncertainly in the car tracks for a moment and then buckled almost at right angles as Robert "Speed" Morris slammed on the brakes and slid the brilliantly painted rattletrap squarely against the curb in front of the Sugar Bowl.

With the screech of the brakes the crowd of boys on the sidewalk looked up and scattered in mock fear and horror, screaming and yelling: "Destry rides again!" "Hi-yo, Silver!" "It's a plane—it's a bird! No! It's SUPERMAN!"

Speed laughed and nudged the tall, blond boy seated at his side. "Okay, pal," he said, "unload the body!"

William "Chip" Hilton grinned and swung his bandaged leg through the space which formerly had been graced by a door. As he limped across the walk he was greeted by: "Hiya, Chip!" "Atta boy, Chip!" "How's the ole pin?"

Hilton greeted them briefly and swung on through

1

the door. Crutches would have helped ease the weight on his leg, but that would have been too much—he just wouldn't do it! Doc Jones had finally consented to their elimination, but Chip didn't know he had been confined an extra ten days because of his distaste for those same crutches.

"Well, if it ain't ole Chipper himself," yelled Petey Jackson delightedly, spilling half the coke he held in his skinny hand. "Hey! Hey! The gang's all here! How's about a little grip of the flipper, kid?"

Little Petey Jackson was the best soda jerk in town. He was older than Chip and had quit school several years earlier to go to work. However, he was a rabid sports fan and extremely popular with the athletes. When Chip had been injured, Petey was one of the first to visit him at the hospital. When Chip had been worried sick about his job at the Sugar Bowl because it meant so much in helping out at home, Petey had volunteered to take care of Chip's work and had been handling both jobs all during Hilton's absence.

Petey pumped Chip's arm and appraised him aloud. "Huh! Pretty soft! Must weigh two hundred pounds. Looks taller, too!" He led Hilton laughing and protesting to the penny scales. "Get on, Big Boy," he said, "we'll see." He dropped a coin in the slot and then affected shocked surprise. "Only one-seventy? Six feet two, and only one-seventy? What'd they feed you up at that repair shop?"

Chip hung on to Petey's hand as they slapped and tugged at one another. It was sure good to be back. . . .

"How ya feelin', pal? When ya comin' back to the ole grind?"

"It's up to the boss; hope it's right away. Where is he?"

"Storeroom, as usual. Go on back."

John Schroeder was the most popular businessman in Valley Falls and was intensely interested in the high school youngsters. His interest went beyond the needs of his drugstore business, for he was well to do and could have retired long ago had he wished. Many people said that he had opened the sweet shop adjoining his drugstore just so the high school kids would have a social center. Others said he did it to keep the youngsters out of the pharmacy. He looked up from his desk as Hilton opened the door, and his surprised expression quickly changed to an enthusiastic smile.

"*Hello*, Chip! Am I glad to see *you!* Come on in here and sit down. How are you feeling anyway?" Without waiting for an answer he grabbed Hilton by the hand and led him over to the desk chair. "Boy, I'll bet you're glad to get out of the house again."

"I sure am, Mr. Schroeder. I want to thank you for coming up to see me and—"

"Tut, tut," broke in the kindly man, "think I wouldn't?"

"No, sir—but—Mr. Schroeder—Mom wanted me to thank you for keeping my pay going. I didn't deserve it."

John Schroeder walked over and gently shoved a half-closed fist against Hilton's jaw. "Now, listen to me, youngster. If you hadn't deserved it, you wouldn't have gotten it. Understand?"

Chip gulped. "I'd like to get back to work if you still want me—"

"Well, you don't think for a minute that anyone could take your place, do you?" Mr. Schroeder smiled. "Sure, you can come back to work—sooner the better! Petey's been doing swell, but he probably has every corner in the place swept full of dust. As for some of those show-cases out there—they haven't been washed for a week!"

"I'll start tonight then, if it's all right with you."

"Sure, start right in. Tonight's a good time."

Hilton did all of the cleaning in the drugstore and the Sugar Bowl. His work consisted of sweeping out, wash-ing the big glass windows, polishing the counters, burning papers, stocking the shelves, unpacking and checking supplies, and boxing shipments. It was a tough job, but it was vital to Chip because it still left him time to do his schoolwork and take part in athletics.

John Schroeder closed both stores at eleven o'clock every night except Saturday, and Hilton started work as soon as the doors were locked. There was only about an hour's cleaning work to be done at night. Chip was allowed to do his other chores at any time of the day most convenient to his personal program. Occasionally, Speed Morris, Taps Browning, or Biggie Cohen would join him in the storeroom and study. Later they would help him "close up."

Chip peeked out the storeroom door. It was just like old times. . . . Speed was sitting on the last chair at the soda counter, intently absorbed in Petey's latest coin-and-glass trick. Out front, Chip could see Fats Ohlsen holding forth. Everything was the same. . . . Closing the door gently, he breathed a sigh of satisfaction and rejoined John Schroeder.

Although several days had passed since Valley Falls had defeated Steeltown for the state football championship of Section Two, the drugstore quarterbacks were still talking about the victory. They grouped in front of the Sugar Bowl every evening and second-guessed the strategy of the coach and even the quarterbacking of Speed Morris—everyone's hero.

Tonight, big, blustering Joel "Fats" Ohlsen, a head taller than anyone present, had the center of the stage. He had singled out Chip Hilton as his pet peeve, and was holding forth aggressively to his particular cronies.

"Well, we won without the great Hilton, didn't we? He thought the team would fall apart when he got hurt. Anyway, he deserved what he got—going high hat with Piggie Thomas after the Delford game!"

"Yeah!" agreed someone. "Yeah, can you imagine that? The janitor of the Sugar Bowl had to ride home in a Packard with society. Why, he was the great Chip Hilton, the star, the captain, the big shot!"

"Too good to come home in the bus with the rest of the team," growled Fats. "Huh! No wonder they had a wreck; probably talked Piggie blind bragging about himself."

"Don't see how you can blame Hilton for the wreck," ventured Stinky Ferris. "Piggie was driving."

"Speedin's the word for it," said Bob Graham.

"Well, he won't drive that particular car very fast again—" Ed Shelton began.

"You mean what's left of it," interrupted Stinky. "Old man Thomas said Piggie couldn't drive for a year— guess he's plenty sore!"

"Hilton fixed everything, didn't he?" growled Ohlsen. "Nearly lost Valley Falls the championship, broke his leg, wrecked Piggie's Packard, and worried his poor mother sick; just because he wanted to be the conquering hero and come riding home ahead of the team."

"Is that so?" drawled a lazy voice.

Biggie Cohen, unnoticed before, had been standing in the shadow of the wall which separated the drugstore from the Sugar Bowl. Now the big football tackle moved slowly over in front of Ohlsen. Placing his hands on his hips he looked straight into Joel's eyes. The others began to press back against the big glass window. Everything about Biggie expressed overpowering emotion.

"Is that so?" he repeated, his black eyes glittering angrily.

Ohlsen grew red, stammered, and vainly tried to find words. "I—I—" he began.

"I know," Biggie growled. "You're a great talker— behind a fellow's back." He flashed forward. Before Fats could move, Biggie had pressed him back against the building.

"Leave Chip Hilton alone! Understand—Fat Stuff?"

"Sure—sure, Biggie," welched Fats.

"Okay, don't forget it!" Biggie disdainfully turned his back on Fats, took a few steps, and then again faced Fats. "In case you don't know it, wise guy, Chip had as much to do with the winning of that game as anyone. He figured out the scoring play that tied the game and got Rock to let Speed drop-kick the winning point."

He turned to the others in the stilled group. "You guys oughta be ashamed of yourselves. Chip plays his heart out in everything he does—and you know it!" His voice was cold and hard.

The group broke up quietly. Biggie had completely spoiled that little round-table discussion.

Joel Ohlsen and Stinky Ferris were almost home before a word was spoken. Suddenly Ohlsen blurted out, "I hate that guy!"

"Biggie?"

"Yeah, him and Hilton both—I'll get even with them if it takes me twenty years!"

Joel's father, Joel Palmer Ohlsen, Sr., was one of the richest men in Valley Falls. As long as anyone in the town could remember, J. P. Ohlsen had been a dominant figure in the town's destiny. Everyone in Valley Falls knew the wealthy and aggressive man as "J. P." Tall, angular, and dictatorial in manner, he ruled his business associates and his employees with an iron hand. Yet, withal, he was eminently fair and just. Joel, Jr., was J. P.'s only son and his only weakness.

J. P. Ohlsen owned the town's biggest lumber- and coalyard, about all the houses in town—everyone said—

and was the president and main stockholder of the pottery, Valley Falls' chief enterprise.

"Biggie's tough," Stinky said hesitantly.

"Yeah?" snarled Joel. "Wait and see! Bigger they are —harder they fall!"

"Think you can lick Biggie?" persisted Stinky.

"You don't think I'm crazy enough to bust one of the town's idols, do you?"

"Don't know—guess you can whip Hilton, though."

"Did it once; I'll do it again, too!"

"Hilton had a bad leg, didn't he?" ventured Stinky. Then he quickly asked, "What've you got against Hilton, anyway? What'd he ever do to you?"

"Plenty! Think I'm gonna forget who started calling me 'Fat Stuff'?"

"What's so serious about that? Heck, Joel, you *are* fat! Anyway, Hilton just did that in fun."

"Yeah? Well, I don't think it's funny. You better watch out how *you* talk, too!" Ohlsen was in an ugly mood, and the two parted in silence.

Completely oblivious of the scene in front of the drugstore, Chip had scarcely moved from his position at Mr. Schroeder's desk when Speed Morris barged through the storeroom door. He was closely followed by Taps Browning. Morris waved a little book at Chip and exploded: "Hey, listen! Listen to this story about Ike Eisenhower."

Chip, accustomed to Speed's violent enthusiasms, slowly turned his head toward Taps and cautiously winked one eye.

Unperturbed by Chip's lack of interest, Morris continued, "Eisenhower went out for football at West Point and broke his leg—" Shaking his head in a determined manner and enunciating each word slowly, he went on, "—and then he became a cheerleader!"

"I don't believe it!" said Chip, swinging his body around and easing his leg up on a chair. "Let's see!"

Chip's eyes were glued to the book but, before he had finished the first page, he was interrupted by Taps.

"Hey!" Taps was standing over him, his head scraping the ceiling light, arms swinging, a veritable flag pole. "Hey, Chip! That gives me an idea! Why don't you try out for basketball manager? Greg Lewis had to quit school—bet you'd get it." Taps was excited.

"Me? A manager?" Chip laughed. "Get out!"

"What's the matter with that?" challenged Speed. Then without waiting for an answer he continued with mock sarcasm: "Oh, the great Chip Hilton—why, he wouldn't *think* of being a manager. Eisenhower could be a cheerleader at West Point, but that's different—he was just an ordinary guy!"

For a moment Chip's temper flared, and his gray eyes narrowed angrily. All the frustration that had gnawed at his heart as he sat in the bleachers during the final game of the recent football season came near to finding an outlet now in bitter words. . . . Speed probably didn't realize how it felt to be barred from sports. . . . Why a fellow burned all up inside just watching. . . . Sitting on the bench was bad enough, but to an athlete the thought of a permanent grandstand seat was unbearable. Slowly regaining his composure, he ventured, "Well, I didn't mean it that way, but—"

"But what?" persisted Speed.

Chip's thoughts ran on . . . Speed was one of his best friends . . . he couldn't quarrel with Speed . . . why, he had shared everything with him . . . they had been classmates ever since they had started school . . . just the same, how could he ask Coach Rockwell to make him manager?

He looked up and then grinned slowly. "But nothing."

"Well, what about it?" persisted Speed. "We gotta have you around some way!"

Chip raised himself to a standing position and thought it over. Maybe it wouldn't be too bad after all . . . might give him something to think about . . . if he got the job . . . at least he wouldn't have to sit in the bleachers. . . .

Shaking his head and eying Speed with distaste he sighed resignedly, "Okay, Mr. Fixit! Okay."

"You mean it?" Speed asked eagerly.

"Sure!"

"Gee, that's swell," breathed Taps.

"Okay, Toots, take a letter!" Speed wasted no time. "To Coach Henry Rockwell, Valley Falls High School: Dear Coach—"

"Wait a minute," interrupted Chip. "Maybe Rock won't want me around after what happened—"

"Forget it. That's ancient history." Speed shook his head impatiently. "Never look over your shoulder, me lad," he quipped. "I'll fix it!"

The next half-hour was a turmoil of suggestions, criticisms, and heated debate, but at last the letter was finished. Speed grabbed it from Chip's reluctant hand and dashed for the door. "Be right back, Chipper, soon as I mail this."

Pivoting quickly, he barged across the room, threw a fake shoulder block at a packing box and half-ran, half-fell, through the door.

"He'll break his neck someday," Taps said.

Chip rumpled his short, blond hair with both hands and rubbed his forehead, reflecting. Speed always knows what he wants and goes after it . . . I wish I were like that. . . .

Later, after the boys had dropped him off at home, Chip pulled Speed's little book from his pocket and continued reading.

Eisenhower nearly lost his leg when he was a kid . . . blood poisoning . . . and he wouldn't let them amputate and it got well . . . and then, just as Speed said, he hurt it again at the Point . . . and when the doctor told him he could never play football again he became a cheerleader. . . . He almost didn't graduate because of his leg. . . .

The book was full of stories of other personalities; most of them were centered around men who had succeeded in sports in spite of physical handicaps.

There was the story of Glenn Cunningham who had been badly burned as a kid and was told that he might never be able to walk . . . but he did! He was told that he would never be able to run . . . but he did! He ran on will power . . . and became the most remarkable runner the world has ever known. . . .

Gregg Rice . . . another great runner . . . the sports world was amazed at his record . . . achieved in the face of a handicap seemingly incurable. . . .

Chip closed his eyes and let his thoughts wander back to the night of his accident. Old Doc Jones had come right away; had worked half the night setting the ankle. Everything had to be just right with Doc . . . good old Doc. He could still hear him saying "Bum leg, nothing —you wait! That leg will be as good as new in six months." Gosh . . . what if he had to limp the rest of his life. . . . Then he could hear Doc saying again "You can do anything—anything you want to do—"

Chip undressed slowly; he was worn out. Getting back on the job and making up his schoolwork had tired him out. He had never dreamed how much the Sugar Bowl and Petey and Mr. Schroeder meant to him. Then, too, he had missed the school crowd that made their headquarters at the store.

Clicking off the light he stretched out in bed, his mind full of thoughts concerning the letter to Coach Rockwell and its possibilities . . . his mother, too . . . her love and hopes. She sure was no quitter. . . .

Mary Hilton was so small and appeared so young that she could have passed for Chip's older sister. Chip and his mother each had a straight nose, a small mouth with thin lips, gray eyes, and the same shade of unruly blond hair.

Every evening Chip would put both arms around his

mother, pick her up, hold her close to his chest, and swing her around in a circle. Mrs. Hilton would struggle and pretend anger. "William Hilton," she would scold, "put me down this instant!"

Chip would let her down then and pretend to be terribly frightened. "I'm sorry, Mom," he would say, and Mrs. Hilton would forgive him with a kiss. They both liked the little game; it was their special way of expressing their love for each other.

Mrs. Hilton was always working and planning for Chip's future. She was determined that he should have a college education, always talking about the day when he would enter State. Nothing he could ever say shook her determination.

"Why, Chip," she would say, "you owe *that* to your father. His greatest hope was that you would go through State."

Just last night they had talked about college again. "But, Mother," Chip had remonstrated, "I'd rather finish high school and go to work. I don't think I could stand it if I had to sit on the side lines. My leg—" He had been silent for a moment. "Besides, you need me here at home."

His mother had checked him then. "We've made out all right so far, son; we'll get along all right when you go to college."

CHAPTER 2

SCRAPBOOK MEMORIES

Chip closed the scrapbook with a snap, crushed the *Yellow Jacket* between his hands, and pushed back from the desk. Grasping the book, he hurled it across the room and glared at Morris.

"Manager of a basketball team! You fixed it all right. Smokes, I must have been crazy to let you talk me into *that!*"

Yes, Speed had fixed it. That day's *Yellow Jacket* had carried the story of Hilton's appointment as basketball manager. Speed had hurried over with the school paper right after school.

Morris closed the book he had been studying and carefully straightened up from his comfortable position on the couch.

"What's eating you now?" he asked, his black eyes studying Chip's scowling face.

"Aw—nothing. I don't know."

14

"What do you mean, you don't know?"

"Oh, I don't know. All my life I've been dreaming of a scholarship at State. Gosh, that would have taken care of a lot of my expenses. Maybe I could have worked and sent some money home to Mom, too. They don't give scholarships to managers, you know."

"They don't give 'em all to athletes, either. You talk like you're the only guy who ever had a broken leg. Most of them heal stronger than ever."

"Could be."

"Could be, nothing. It's true!"

"S'pose it doesn't? What then? You think I'm going up to State and let my mother slave for four years?"

"You could get a job. I'll have to work. We'll both work!"

"Nope, I'm not going to waste four years. I'll get a job in the pottery—probably where I belong, anyway."

"Look, Chip, college is nearly two years away. We've got this year and then our senior year before college. Let's forget about it until after graduation. Okay?"

"Guess so. Well," Chip gestured toward the scrapbook and the scattered clippings, "guess I'd better buy some post cards and change that thing to a photograph album."

"That leg's only gonna need a little rest and time. Quit beefin'! Bet you're playing baseball by spring. Anyway, there's more to school than athletics!"

"Coming from you, that's good!" exclaimed Chip, moving dejectedly toward the door where the scrapbook lay in a heap on the floor.

"Jeeps!" shouted Speed, glancing at his watch, "I'm late for supper! Mom'll kill me!"

He grabbed his coat with one hand, brushed his thick black hair back with the other, and dashed out the door. "Hate to leave you, toots, but I'm late already." Speed was looking back over his shoulder and talking as he ran.

Chip watched Speed turn at the end of the hall and swing out the front door. Speed's footwork always amazed him, but this afternoon it struck home hard. Speed had been the only player on the squad who gave him any competition when Coach Rockwell called for a race the length of the football field.

Speed would jump the gun and be in the lead for the first fifty yards; then Chip's long strides would begin to tell, and he would slowly creep up and take the lead ten yards from the goal line—always close—seemed like he and Speed had always pushed each other. . . .

Sitting at the study desk Chip read the clipping slowly and reflectively. He had cut the article from the sports page of the Valley Falls *Yellow Jacket*. Gee whiz . . . he hadn't even thanked Speed for bringing the paper over. . . .

Once more he looked at the clipping. By now he had almost memorized the contents:

FORMER VARSITY STAR APPOINTED
BASKETBALL MANAGER

William "Chip" Hilton, a member of the junior class and a star center on last year's basketball team, will serve as varsity basketball manager this year.

Hilton was injured several weeks ago in an automobile accident. He was co-captain of the football team and a great passer and kicker.

Hilton's injury keeps him out of a basketball uniform, but the team will be fortunate in having an experienced basketball player as manager.

Chip is the son of the famous William "Big Chip" Hilton, All-American football and basketball player, who played at the Valley Falls High before going to State University. Mr. Hilton, formerly chief chemist at the Valley Falls Pottery, was killed in an accident there several years ago.

Frank Watts and Herbert Holden were named assistant basketball managers.

Chip laid the heavy scrapbook on the desk at his side and pasted in the clipping. Somehow it looked insignificant among all those empty black pages he had hoped to fill with his junior-year clippings. The fact that the first half of the book bulged with glowing accounts of his freshman and sophomore years served only to dishearten him. Headlines, and sometimes whole columns of type, told of his athletic feats and record-breaking accomplishments.

Turning the pages, he glanced at the headlines and relived every thrilling moment they recalled: "Valley Falls Wins, Chip Hilton Stars" . . . "Hilton and Morris Selected for East-West All-High Game" . . . "Morris and Hilton Chosen All-State" . . . "Hilton and Morris, Three-Letter Stars, Attend Spring Practice at State."

Hilton had earned six letters at Valley Falls High before his junior year. "Guess that's the end of that," he murmured.

A familiar stride on the front porch brought him out of his reverie. The door opened and in the dim hall only Taps Browning's shoulders were visible. Then with a duck of his head he was in the room. "Hiya, manager," he beamed, waving a copy of the *Yellow Jacket* in the air. "See the paper?" Taps was exuberant. His blue eyes sparkled behind his silver-rimmed spectacles.

"Yes, I saw it. Speed brought it over."

"Boy, that's the best news that's been in the paper this year! How you feelin'?"

"Okay—except for this manager stuff. Don't know whether that's good or not, Taps." Suddenly his mood changed and with a grin he added, "Anyway, I guess I won't have to pay my way into the games."

Taps sensed Chip's feelings and said quickly, "You sure won't, Chip. The gang's been pulling hard for you. The team needs someone like you. You'll be a help to all of us—specially me!" Grasping Chip gently by the arms he added, "I'm glad you're going to be manager, Chip. Maybe now I'll be able to make the team. I don't know what I'd do if you weren't around. Gosh, it doesn't seem that it was only this fall that we met out there on the Hilton A. C. court, remember? You taught me more basketball—"

The tall youngster broke off suddenly to protect himself from a good-natured, though threatening, gesture from his friend.

"Cut the sob stuff, kid," growled Chip.

"Well, see you in the morning, Chip—gotta stay home tonight. Mom said she wanted to see what I look like. Night!"

"Twenty-two, twenty-three, twenty-four."

Chip stopped counting and paused for a rest . . . this was hard to take. He was breathing heavily and he was glad he had reached the landing. Come to think of it, this was the first time he had been up the gym steps since before the Steeltown football game. . . .

Boy, how about that! He had never even noticed counting steps before. Now, he bet he knew how many steps there were between every floor in Valley Falls High.

There was a certain something in the air today which Chip sensed instinctively. It was the approach of winter—and basketball. Yes, basketball was in the air! His pulse quickened.

He looked back down the long flight of steps. Funny, he had never realized before how many steps there were leading to the gym. Glancing at the huge gym door, he started upward again, counting as he climbed . . . twenty-five, -six, -seven, -eight, -nine . . . thirty. The big door required no small effort to open, and he was glad to find himself inside. He paused inside the big foyer, a bit out of breath; as he used to be after he'd dashed up these same steps, three at a time.

Arriving in front of Coach Rockwell's office, Chip stopped for a few seconds to collect his wits before knocking. He knew a lot about this office. Every inch of space on the walls was covered with pictures of teams and great players who had played for Coach Rockwell and Valley Falls down through the years. His dad's picture was up there; maybe his would be up there, too, someday. Right now, though, he was more concerned with his appointment with Coach Rockwell. Well . . . might as well get it over with. . . .

A hearty "Come in!" greeted his knock, and he found himself face to face with Coach Rockwell. Chip stood there tongue-tied. In the hospital and even at the championship football game, when Coach Rockwell had asked him to sit up in the stands and help figure out the weakness in Steeltown's defense, he had tried unsuccessfully to work up enough nerve to unburden his feelings; to tell the Rock how sorry he was for breaking a team rule after the Delford game.

Chip had mentally rehearsed this meeting many times and doped out just what he would say. It wasn't because the Valley Falls head coach was someone to be afraid of or the kind of man a boy couldn't talk to freely. Not at all. In the many years Rockwell had taught football, basketball, baseball, and sportsmanship to successive generations of boys at Valley Falls High he had become a town institution. A strict disciplinarian, he demanded the best a fellow had in him at all times. The boys on his teams grumbled over the long, extra hours of practice which he required, but a

Rockwell-coached athlete was welcomed on every college campus. Coach Henry Rockwell was a perfectionist.

The Rock knew boys inside and out. He knew, for instance, what had been troubling Chip ever since the disaster that followed the Delford game more than a month ago. He had no patience with members of his teams who broke his rules. He knew Chip had had a good reason. If only the boy had told him why he had to get back to town early. . . . But a youngster like Chip wouldn't betray a confidence. He had taken the consequences. And now the kid was worried because he had put his coach in the position of showing favoritism to a player who had broken a rule. Well, the Rock had been a sensitive lad once himself. Coach Rockwell shook himself out of his reverie and looked up.

"Why, hello, Chip. Come in, sit down." Rockwell's face was friendly, and he smiled a little as he quizzed, "Been worrying about this little meeting?"

Chip was relieved by the friendly greeting, and all his uncertainty vanished. "Yes, I have, Coach—but I've been wanting to tell you how sorry—"

"Let's forget it, Chip. Okay? After all—we won the championship!"

"Yes, but, Coach—"

"Chip!" There was a note of finality in Rockwell's voice. "What's done is done!" He leaned back in his chair and regarded the tall youngster with friendly black eyes. "I know just how you feel, Chip. *Exactly* how you feel. And I know the whole story, too, about that night you got a lift in Piggie's car. In your shoes and in the same situation, I probably would have done precisely as you did. What say we forget about it and start all over in basketball? Okay?"

Chip's throat was a bit tight, but the deep breath he took cleared away the feeling and he managed a faint "Sure, Coach."

The big leather chair squeaked a bit as Rockwell swung it toward the window and shifted his eyes out over Ohlsen Stadium. The room was quiet while Coach Rockwell's thoughts flew back over the years. To other years when another tall, blond, youngster with level, gray eyes had sat in front of his desk. . . . They had called that other boy Chip, too. . . .

Again the leather chair protested as Rockwell turned back to his desk. "Leg bother you much now?"

"No, sir, at least not too much."

"I'm glad to hear that! I saw Doc Jones yesterday and he said it was coming along fine. Doc tells me that he's fixing you up with one of his trick braces tomorrow. That old guy knows more about bones than any big shot in the surgical profession. If he were located in some big city he'd be a bone specialist with a big rep. Here he's just old Doc Jones." The coach was silent for a moment. Then he nodded reassuringly and added, "It'll come along all right in time."

"I sure hope so," Chip said earnestly, "I'd give my right arm to play one more year of football."

"You will, Chip. You've got a lot of football left."

Coach Rockwell spoke in such a friendly tone that

for a moment Chip forgot himself. "I always dreamed of playing at State!"

Coach Rockwell broke in quickly. "You will, Chip. I wrote to State about you and Speed even before they had you up for their reception last spring."

The coach rubbed his clean-shaven chin and studied the tall youngster with keen eyes. "What course are you taking?"

"General, Coach."

"What are you going to study in college?"

"I was planning to go to State and study chemistry—" Chip stopped suddenly. He had nearly added, "—if my leg is okay."

"Ceramics," queried Rockwell, "like your dad?"

"Yes." Chip finished lamely. "But I had journalism in mind, too."

"What kind of journalism? News? Sports?"

"Sports, I guess. I like sports stories."

"No reason you shouldn't be anything you want to be, Chip. You *can* be anything you want to be, a ceramic chemist like your father, a sports writer like Joe Kennedy or Pete Williams, or a physician like Doc Jones. But there's time for all that later. The main thing right now is doing good work in high school—and really learning basketball," he added, smiling.

Coach Rockwell moved quickly from his chair to a bookcase near the files. Glancing rapidly along a shelf, he grasped a black-bound book. "Here's a book you should read: Naismith's *History of Basketball*. Take it along and bring it back when you've finished." He paused a moment. "You'll get a lot of basketball out of that little book, no matter whether you plan to be a coach, a sports writer, or what!"

Chip felt a glow of confidence now, and his heart was beating rapidly as the coach went on, "Naismith's book will give you a good background for basketball, and it contains a lot of interesting dope that's not generally known."

"I hope I can do a good job as manager, Coach."

"You will. You've played the game, and you've had more responsibilities than most boys your age. By the way, will this manager's job interfere with your job at the Sugar Bowl?"

"Oh, no, sir. No, sir!"

"I'm glad of that. I know one thing sure, Chip. If your dad were in your shoes he'd be right in there pitching, giving all he had for the team, whether he was the star, a sub on the bench, or the manager!"

Pointing to the book Chip was holding, he continued, "The man who wrote that book and who invented basketball had the right spirit. Naismith showed a lot of courage when he went in for physical education and athletics. He had to buck everybody—his friends, his only sister, the church, and his teachers. But he felt, like most coaches who love their work, that no man can have a better job than the opportunity to work with youngsters and help them develop into real men."

Chip was silent for a moment. Then, getting back to his own problem, he said hesitantly, "I don't know much about being a manager, Coach."

The corners of Coach Rockwell's thin lips twisted into a half-smile as he regarded the boy quizzically. "You didn't know much about football either, four or five years ago, did you, Chip?"

Chip smiled and scratched his head. "I sure didn't!" Suddenly he felt sure of himself and made a mental resolution. He'd be the best manager Valley Falls ever had . . . if it killed him. . . . Eisenhower could be a cheerleader . . . well, Chip Hilton could be a manager. . . . A good one!

CHAPTER 3

A CHIP OFF
THE OLD BLOCK

Downstairs in the big living room Speed, Biggie, Red, and Ted Williams were singing. Mrs. Hilton was playing her old-time favorites and the boys were harmonizing and generally having fun. Although Ross Montgomery never sang, Chip could visualize him sitting beside Mrs. Hilton on the piano bench, following the music. Pretty soon, when she got tired, Ross would take over.

Then the keys would really talk! Ross was talented and could play any type of music well. Chip guessed he liked his mother's playing best, though. It seemed more homelike . . . more natural. . . .

Chip was concentrating on an English theme which Mr. Wilkinson wanted at his next class. Naismith's book on basketball had provided some good material for the composition, and Chip had jotted down a number of facts which he felt would be interesting.

Basketball was a natural. What else could he have put his heart into this evening? Nothing! Basketball was surging through his veins.

Chip made passing marks in English, but it was always a struggle. His thoughts wandered away from the composition, and he began to think of his future. If he had trouble with a little English paper, how could he ever be a sports writer?

Ross Montgomery was playing now and suddenly the gang burst into a rapid rendition of "Old MacDonald's" tricky lyrics. This was a song they all knew, and the words rang out loud and clear:

"Old MacDonald had a farm, EE-YI, EE-YI, OH,
    And on this farm he had some chicks, EE-YI,
    EE-YI, OH!
With a chick-chick here, a chick-chick there,
Here a chick, there a chick, everywhere a chick-
    chick,
Old MacDonald had a farm, EE-YI, EE-YI, OH!"

Chip laid aside his composition and listened intently. The melody was old and familiar, but he had some words of his own that were running through his mind in time with the music:

"Old Chip Hilton has a leg, EE-YI, EE-YI, OH,
    And on this leg he has a brace, EE-YI, EE-YI,
    OH!
With a limp-limp here, a limp-limp there,

Here a limp, there a limp, everywhere a limp-
limp,
Old Chip Hilton has a limp, EE-YI, EE-YI, OH!"

His thoughts turned suddenly to Doc Jones and he
imagined the words "Old Patch-'Em-Up" would have
substituted:

"Old Chip Hilton has a brace, EE-YI, EE-YI, OH,
But someday this brace will go, EE-YI, EE-YI,
OH,
And when it goes, he'll never know, EE-YI, EE-YI,
OH!"

Can't come too soon, he mused. Here . . . how about
Wilkie's composition? He again tried to concentrate on
the paper, but it was no use. Despite every effort to
study, his thoughts turned to the basketball team and
the part he might play in its success. Greg Lewis had
been manager for the last two years and had gone on
the trips, kept score, and handed out the equipment.
There didn't seem to be any way to be outstanding in
that kind of job. . . .

Speed's raucous shout broke his reverie. "Hey, book-
worm, come on down. What ya doing? Tomorrow's
Saturday, and you can study all day."

"Wonder what kind of job he thinks I've got," Chip
muttered. "Okay," he called. "Be right down." He might
as well go down with the gang—he couldn't concentrate
with all that noise anyway.

The big living room was crowded. Every chair, sofa, and even the floor, was occupied. Everyone greeted Chip as he entered with, "Hiya, kid!" "Hello, manager."

Ross Montgomery was sitting at his usual place on the piano bench. "What'd Coach say?" he asked.

"Oh, he gave me a real going-over. Talked mostly about my job and then went into the career act."

"He would!" Ted Williams laughed. Ted was president of the senior class. He was so shy and quiet that it was hard to realize that he was a star football player.

"The slave driver!" grunted Red Schwartz.

Chip agreed mentally. Coach Rockwell was a slave driver when it came to coaching, but the players all seemed to like it! He sure had . . . even that time last fall when the Rock had bawled him out. . . .

"See Rogers?" queried Red.

"No."

"Rogers is the only man alive who can get Rock's goat," said Speed.

Burrell Rogers was faculty manager of athletics. However, he seldom concerned himself with coaching, but confined his activities to administrative work.

"Who's really the boss—Rock or Rogers?" Biggie asked.

"Huh!" snorted Speed. "Nobody bosses Rock except the Board of Education. Most of *them* are scared of him. Rock is an institution."

"I don't think he's very optimistic about this year's material," Chip said.

"Look," said Speed. "Rock always uses that line. We

won't have many out for the team this year, but what of it?"

"Hampton'll have more out for their team than we have in the whole senior class," laughed Red.

"Well, Coach doesn't do so bad with what he gets," broke in Biggie. "He's won more championships than all the rest of the coaches in the state put together, I guess."

"He said the schedule was the toughest in the history of the school," said Chip.

"That's him, all right," said Red. "Always worrying. Rock waves the biggest crying-towel in the state!"

"He's a great moaner," agreed Ross, securing himself more firmly on the piano bench, "but I can't see any need to cry about this year's basketball prospects. Gosh, there's Red, Speed here, Buzz Todd, Soapy Smith, and Taps—what more does he want?"

"It's sure surprising the interest some people we know show in sports," observed Chip, "even though they profess to doubt their value."

Ross stood up and shook his head ruefully. "I'd better go. I'm in a den of athletes!"

"I've got to go, too," said Speed. "Don't worry, gang, we'll have a good team. We've got the best coach in the state, and the first all-state manager in the history of basketball."

"Huh!" growled Chip, clumping up the stairs to get his coat before leaving for the Sugar Bowl.

Chip paused outside the open door of Coach Rockwell's office. The Rock, Burrell Rogers, and Assistant

Coach Chet Stewart were seated at the big table. Waiting uncertainly, Chip was relieved when Coach Rockwell looked up and greeted him with a smile. "Come in, Chip."

Chip entered and laid the black book Rockwell had loaned him on the desk. "Here's the book, Coach. Thanks a lot. It was swell."

"Good! I'm glad you liked it."

Chip had never had much contact with Burrell Rogers, but Chet Stewart had been his backfield coach in football and had worked with Coach Rockwell in teaching him basketball for the past two years. Chip knew him well and liked him. He was thrilled at the thought of becoming a part of Valley Falls' board of basketball strategy.

"Sit down next to Chet," continued Coach Rockwell. "You two will have to work pretty close together, you know."

Chip smiled. "Hope I can help," he said.

"We'll need a lot of help with the schedule Rogers pulled out of his hat for us this year." Coach Rockwell was serious now. "It's a suicide schedule for a small squad, and it begins to look as if that's what we'll have."

"First team'll be all right, Coach," interrupted Chet Stewart.

"Not unless we find a center, Chet. A lot depends upon the new candidates. Especially Hilton's protégé, Browning." Coach Rockwell smiled at Chip. "If he only has half your fight, kid, he'll be okay!"

Chip suddenly felt a heavy sense of responsibility.

Speed was right, he reflected, he said this job was a tough one . . . boy . . . wouldn't it be great if Taps could make the team. . . . Maybe I can help a little there, anyway. . . . Guess I know Taps better than anyone . . . he'll make this team or my name's not Hilton. . . . Glad he lives next door, handy to the Hilton A. C. . . . The Hilton A. C. . . . I'll always be grateful to Dad for putting up that backboard and hoop . . . and the football goal posts and the pitcher's rubber. . . . Gosh, Dad had wanted me to be a good athlete. . . . I guess I know now how he felt. . . . I feel the same way about Taps.

"Maybe Browning will develop," Stewart said hopefully. "He's got everything a pivot player needs—height, long arms, and he's a pretty good jumper."

Rockwell laughed. "How do *you* know so much about him?"

It was Stewart's turn to smile. "I've been hearing about Hilton's find from every kid on the block. Chip's been working with him in the Hilton back yard every day. I think Chip's got something!"

Rockwell sighed. "I hope so! We sure need a big man!" He stood up abruptly. "Let's see the movies."

"Good," beamed Rogers. "Pop's got the Weston film all set."

Rogers led the way out of the office and Chip hobbled along beside Chet Stewart. "How's Pop?" he asked.

"Pop? You know Pop—he's *always* all right. What a worker! Takes care of the locker room, the gym, acts as the trainer, and does about everything ten other guys should do!"

"Say, how old is Pop?"

"Well, he's been here at Valley Falls for thirty-five years but that doesn't mean much. Your guess is as good as mine."

Chet quickened his pace to catch up with Rogers and Rockwell. Chip clumped along after him.

The stiff formality of Rogers' office was in sharp contrast to the warmth and fellowship of the room they had just left. Pop smiled broadly as they entered the room. The little stoop-shouldered man was dressed carefully in a blue suit. Holy smokes, thought Chip, I never thought of it before . . . Pop dresses better than Coach!

"All set, Pop?" asked Rogers.

"Yes, sir!" The old fellow smiled. "Rarin' to go!"

"All right, let's go."

Pop pulled down the blinds while the others seated themselves on each side of the big desk. The semidarkness was suddenly broken by a shaft of light as Pop clicked on the projector and they were carried right into last year's Weston game. Chip had played in that game . . . last year a regular on the varsity . . . this year a manager. . . .

When the picture was finished, Rockwell and Rogers said good-bye and filed out of the office, each busy with his own thoughts.

Chet Stewart stretched himself, grabbed old Pop affectionately by the arm, and said, "Pop, Chip's our new manager!"

"Yes, sir, I know that, Mr. Chet. Chip off the old block, Chipper is."

"Sure is," agreed Chet. "Say, I've got to move! Mind, Chip? See you Monday! Four o'clock!"

Chip helped Pop box up the machine and take down the screen. Then they walked down the hall toward the gym lobby. Just before they reached the big door leading to the outside steps, Chip hesitated a moment and looked around. The big foyer was lined with cases containing trophies, plaques, stuffed and varnished footballs, basketballs, and row after row of baseballs—all indicative of Valley Falls victories and championships. Suddenly Chip turned and limped over to a closed case which housed several lacquered basketballs. One ball in particular always held his interest.

"Bet I know what you're looking at, Chipper." Pop shuffled over to the trophy case, adding, "The basketball the team gave Mr. Big Chip!"

"That's right, Pop!"

"That basketball there," Pop continued, "you're lookin' at was the first state championship ball Valley Falls ever won. Your pop won that there championship practically all by himself."

"It's really something when a team feels that way about a fellow, isn't it?"

"Sure is!" Old Pop twisted his head a bit and queried, "Say, Chipper, you had any more trouble with that nogood Fats guy?"

"No, Pop. Not lately."

"Well, Chipper, don't you forget—I trained some mighty good fighters in my time and I can fix you up— no foolin'."

Chip laughed, and before he realized it he found himself back on street level. He didn't even remember limping down the steps. He was thinking about that championship basketball and the player who had done most to win it—his dad.

Mike Sorelli was in a gay mood. The Academy was thronged, and on every table the little brown leather jugs were sending their dancing pills clattering across the green felt time and time again. Kelly pool was a popular game with the pottery workers at any time, but on Saturdays, the day after payday, the stakes were high and the house take mounted fast. Sometimes there were so many players at one table that those who drew a high pill never had a chance to shoot.

Joel Ohlsen liked to drop into the Academy on Saturdays, but he was careful to park his car by the Ferris home in the next block. His father seldom looked right or left when he was driven to and from the pottery, but Joel didn't care to risk being seen.

The crowd from the pottery was not too fond of Joel. But the workers didn't mind getting a little of J. P.'s money without working for it, even though they did say it was like taking candy from a baby. Fats could make a show of his money here and buy a certain amount of attention even when he lost—which was most of the time.

Mike greeted Joel with a smile and waved toward the back of the room. "They're just starting on table nine, Ohlsen, if you want to play—"

It was nearly midnight before Ohlsen had lost all the money he had in his pocket, and nearly one o'clock when he made his way on tiptoe up the stairs to his room. J. P. was always early to bed and early to rise, and Joel knew the dressing down he would get if he were heard coming in at this hour.

Although Mrs. Ohlsen often pleaded with Joel to come home early, she never told J. P. about his late hours. On the few occasions J. P. missed him, Joel had said he was studying at Stinky's. This was always a safe alibi. The Ferris family could not afford a telephone, and J. P. never went to the flats after dark, except when there was an emergency at the plant.

As Joel stood before his bathroom mirror brushing his teeth, the image reflected in the glass wore a sullen look. Why did he keep on hanging around Sorelli's dump when everyone kept taking him for a ride? . . . Why did everyone pick on him all the time . . . fellows like Chip Hilton? . . . Gosh, they used to play together from morning to night when they were kids. . . . He'd licked Chip in a fair fight, hadn't he. . . .

Something stirred in the boy's memory. . . . After all, he was the one who had built up that quarrel and kept it alive . . . and the fight, well, he wasn't too proud of his end of it . . . still, Chip did have all the luck. . . . That smashed leg? . . . Yes, but the guy had it coming to him. . . .

Why should everybody make a hero of Hilton? . . . After all, just because his dad had been an All-American, why should Chip throw his weight around? . . .

Did people think you were nobody if you didn't wear a big VF and be a slave to that conceited Rockwell? . . . Why be a kid all your life? . . . a fellow had to be a man of the world these days. . . .

What right did birds like Chip and Biggie and all those bohunks at the pottery have to look down on an Ohlsen . . . and why did he always have to lose at Kelly pool with all those bums laughing at him?

Joel Ohlsen turned off the light and climbed into bed feeling very sorry for himself. Someday he'd get even with the whole crowd, but even this realization was of small comfort as he lay there wide awake in the dark.

CHAPTER 4

THREE-MAN
BASKETBALL

THE big table was loaded with steaming food, and Mrs. Hilton was hovering over the boys, pretending to be worried about their appetites. Mary Hilton didn't talk much, but Chip's pals would have been amazed at her knowledge of their problems, habits, and ambitions.

Once or twice a week, usually on Friday evenings and sometimes on Sunday afternoons, Chip would invite some of the boys over for dinner. And what a dinner it would be! Mrs. Hilton was second to none when it came to cooking. Today Chip had invited the three basketball veterans—Speed, Red Schwartz, and Buzz Todd. Taps Browning and Soapy Smith didn't need invitations—they had just barged in. Mrs. Browning declared that Taps was the star boarder at the Hilton home.

Table talk ranged from exams, term papers, notebooks, to teachers. After dinner and after dishes—here

Taps and Soapy were the goats—everything centered on sports.

"How's it feel to be through with football, Speed?" asked Taps.

"Plenty good!"

"Going out for basketball right away?"

"Sure!" Speed looked at Taps in surprise. "Why not?"

"Thought you might be tired—"

"I never get tired!" Speed was emphatic.

"Well, a week's rest wouldn't do you any harm," interposed Soapy.

"Yes, and you might get stale," ventured Taps.

"You gotta be good to be stale," flashed Speed.

"Rock says staleness is due to a tired mind," volunteered Red Schwartz.

"That lets Speed out." Soapy grinned. "He doesn't have to worry about brain fatigue."

"What brain?" challenged Red.

Speed remained smilingly unperturbed by the laughter which accompanied the needling.

Buzz Todd changed the subject. "See the Rock yesterday, Chip?" he asked.

"Sure did!"

"Do any manager's work?"

"No, but we looked at the pictures of last year's Weston game and Coach gave me the low-down on my job. Looks tough!"

"You'll soon find out!" Red Schwartz shook his head as he spoke. "Greg had to do everything—set up the tickets, the passes, take charge of the ticket money, wrap ankles, keep score, help Pop with rubdowns, check equipment, and a thousand other things—to say nothing of putting up with Rock when he went temperamental."

"He gave me an outline," continued Chip. "I think Greg must have been four other guys," he added with a long sigh.

"Four other guys is right," agreed Red. "Greg took a lot of punishment from Rock."

"Rock isn't so bad," interrupted Speed. "He might bawl a guy out once in a while, but no one else better do it."

"Yeah," agreed Red. "When Coach is with you, he's with you!"

"Speaking of that," said Speed, "remember last year when Rock and Jenkins tangled? 'Member, Chip?"

"I saw that game," said Soapy. "What was wrong with those guys?"

"It was all on account of Greg," said Speed.

"What happened?" asked Taps.

"It's a long story. Chip, you tell it."

"No, you tell it," protested Chip.

"Go ahead, Speed," urged Buzz.

"You really want to hear it? Heck, *you* fellows were there!"

"I never did know the inside story," said Soapy.

"Aw, let's coax him, girls," mimicked Red.

"Okay! Okay!" laughed Speed. "I'll give." The boys listened attentively. "Greg was keeping score, as you know," he continued, "and it was a tough game. Delford's high scorer was a guy by the name of Bartlett and he was 'hot.' Nobody could hold him. Coach knew Bartlett was weak on the defense and told Chip to keep cutting and to go under the basket and to use two-hand sweep shots to draw fouls."

"That isn't really fair, is it?" Taps was perplexed.

"Nothing wrong with it," said Speed. "Look!" He imitated the underhand sweep shot. "It's a shot that's hard to guard and if it isn't stopped it's an easy two points.

"Chip murdered him. Five minutes after the second half started, Bartlett had four personal fouls."

"Wonder why Coach Jenkins let Bartlett guard Chip?" asked Buzz. "Chip's the best pivot player in the state."

Chip laughed. "Thanks for the roses, pal."

"Well, they did switch him to Tim Murphy," continued Speed, "and then it was really bad. Right off the bat Timmy cut under the basket and scored. Bartlett left him alone a couple more times, and Timmy scored both times. Then he fouled him again, and that was curtains; he was out of the game."

"Greg blew the scorekeeper's horn, jumped to his feet, and held up five fingers." Chip was excited by the memory.

Speed laughed and broke in. "The referee waved Bartlett out of the game—and then the fun began. Coach Jenkins rushed straight across the floor and began to pound the timekeeper's table with his fist and yell that Greg was a crook; that Bartlett had only four fouls; that it was a put-up job; and that Valley Falls was stealing the game. Boy! Was he hot!"

"But how about the scorebooks?" broke in Soapy. "Don't the home-team and visiting-team scorebooks have to check?"

"Sure, and they did. It wouldn't have made any difference if they hadn't, though—the home scorebook is the official book."

"What did Jenkins say to that?" asked Taps.

"Why. believe it or not, he accused Greg of marking an extra foul against Bartlett when Greg checked the two books at half time. The Delford manager was too scared to say anything.

"That's when Greg got sore. I can remember yet— Greg got up and said, 'You can't say that about me,' and then," Speed laughed at the memory, "Coach Jenkins shoved him, and Greg fell right over backward and lit on his back and there he was—feet sticking right up in the air back of the table."

"What did the Rock do?" asked Taps.

"Plenty!" broke in Red. "I had a ringside seat for that one. Chip and Tim Murphy had to pull those two guys apart; they haven't spoken since!"

"How about that!" marveled Taps. "How did it all end?"

"Oh, we finished the game—if you could call it that," said Speed.

"What happened?"

"Well, after they lost Bartlett we got a big lead on

'em, and then they really started roughing it up."

"That's Delford every time," someone said.

"The officials were calling fouls right and left," continued Speed, "and pretty soon both teams were down to their last five men. Then, with about ten minutes to go, Delford lost their fifth man on personals and had only four players left. Rock offered to let the fifth man stay in the game, but Jenkins wouldn't have any part of that. He was sore, and you could hear him ravin' all over the place. Said he expected that kind of officiating at Valley Falls; that Delford couldn't win if ten men played."

"He's a big crybaby," Buzz grunted.

"He's that all right," nodded Red.

"Rock was too smart for Jenkins, though," continued Speed. "He left only four of us in the game, too; four Valley Falls players against four Delford men! But that was nothing! About two minutes later Delford lost another man and that left them with only three players on the floor. Then Coach took me out, and that's the way the game ended—Chip and Hal Bird and Tim Murphy against three of the Delford men —three against three."

"Who won?" asked Taps.

"We did. The tip-off on the game was the fact that, for the first time I can remember, Rock didn't give us a pep talk between halves. You see, Delford used the dressing room right next to ours, and Jenkins hollered and screamed at the Delford gang all through the intermission. Coach just sat down with the rest of us and listened—and then when Jenkins finished he said, 'Well, boys, I can't compete with that act. Let's go!' "

"He didn't give a pep talk at all?" asked Taps.

"Nope!"

"How bad'd you beat them?"

"Ten, fifteen points—something like that."

"Jenkins sure hates the Rock," said Chip. "Every time we play them he puts on a show." He stood up and started out of the room.

"Where do you think you're going?" asked Taps.

"Got to get down to the Sugar Bowl and clean up the joint. It's pretty near eleven o'clock."

"Reminds me," said Red. "I've got two notebooks past due."

Speed startled them all by crashing the piano keys. "Guess we all better do some studying," he said.

An hour later, Chip's chores at the Sugar Bowl having been completed with young Browning's help, Taps closed the front door quietly and followed Chip through the dimly lit hall and up the stairs. Chip sat down at his study table and shuffled through some papers. "Here's that English theme I was telling you about," he said.

"All finished?"

"Just about. It's terrible!"

Taps sat on the bed, reading the paper and unlacing his shoes. "Guess I might as well stay all night," he muttered, "folks are all asleep." He read in silence. After a few minutes he looked up and nodded his head enthusiastically.

"Say, this is good! Where'd you get all the dope?"

"From the book Coach Rockwell loaned me."

"Well, you've sure got a lot of stuff here I never knew about basketball. It's okay!" As he slipped under the covers, he added, "That oughta go in the *Yellow Jacket!*"

"I got a kick out of writing it," said Chip.

Chip doused the lights and crawled into bed. A little later he heard his mother's footsteps stop in the hall outside the door. She had come to see if he was all right. Even though she retired early, Mrs. Hilton could never rest until Chip was home safe in bed.

CHAPTER 5

NICKNAMES WIN
GAMES

Taps paced his steps with Chip's slow limp as the two friends neared the school. At the foot of the long, stone steps Biggie Cohen joined them.

"Hiya, Chipso. Hiya, Taps."

On their way up the steps Taps and Biggie held back so that Chip's progress would not be hastened. Steps were not so much of a handicap now . . . Doc's brace was something! Sometimes he hardly realized it was there. . . .

As they neared the top flight, Joel Ohlsen and Stinky Ferris caught up with them.

"Ha, pipe the sympathy act, Stinky," snickered Fats. "Looks like the athletes can't take it."

Chip ignored the digs completely, but Taps squared his shoulders and took a deep breath. Taps looked seven feet tall as he clenched his fists, stopped, and glared at his fat tormentor.

"Come on, Taps, skip it!" Chip grasped Taps by the arm.

Ohlsen and Ferris had reached the top landing and as he opened the front door, Joel couldn't resist a final dig. "Don't rush, Stinky. School can't possibly start till the number one grandstander arrives."

Chip's blood boiled. There was cold loathing in the gray eyes he lifted toward Ohlsen. "Someday that big mouth of yours will show up with some teeth missing, Fat Stuff."

"You'll never see that day, grandstander. You—nor any of your alley friends." Joel turned his mocking eyes deliberately toward Biggie and moved through the door.

Biggie made a quick move toward the door and then stopped. His tight lips and squared jaw indicated the effort he was exerting to control himself. Then, drawing a deep breath, he unclenched his hands and shook his head. "Someday I'm gonna smash his face in," he muttered.

That afternoon Chip hurried down to the dressing room. Stopping in the doorway of Pop's training room he sniffed the air appreciatively. To an athlete, the most wonderful perfume in the world is that intangible dressing-room aroma which accumulates from liniment, wintergreen, rubbing alcohol, and witch hazel. Boy, oh boy . . . back again at practice. This was more like it! . . . .

A few minutes later he clumped up the stairs to the gym. Coach Rockwell was sitting up on the top row of

the bleachers, his sharp, black eyes shifting from player
to player. The coach looked fit all right. He was dressed
in a plain, gray, warm-up track suit, but it couldn't
conceal his muscular build. Chip had never thought
much about the Rock's size, nor his age . . . guess he
was pressing sixty, all right, but he didn't look it. His
hair was still black and he had most of it. He stood
above five feet ten and he could handle his one hundred
and eighty pounds like a cat. He was compact and well
proportioned. When practice was under way, the Rock
worked as hard as the players, his eyes darting here and
there, never missing a trick.

Chip wondered if he had forgotten anything. "I guess
not," he murmured to himself. "Balls all pumped up,
Rock's little public address system all set, ready to be
snapped on, players' shoes fitted, practice gear issued. . . ."

Valley Falls' new hopefuls, all equipped with white
trunks, T-shirts, practice shoes, socks, were—as Pop
would say—"rarin' to go."

Chip had been sitting in the bleachers opposite Coach
Rockwell, watching the boys warm up before practice
time. The hands on the big gym clock showed five
minutes to four o'clock. Although the coach had been
working with the veterans for the past week, this was
the first formal practice of the season.

Chip's eyes ranged over the squad. Most of the try-
outs were small. In fact, they looked like grade school
kids. Valley Falls' team would be small this year, he
was thinking. There were only two players taller than

six-two, Taps and Bill English, a freshman who was six-three.

The gang really felt good—and showed it—cutting up, shouting, slapping, stealing the ball from one another, running aimlessly here and there, and passing and shooting carelessly without pattern or purpose.

Watching the fellows warm up, Chip had not noticed that the big clock showed one minute after four o'clock and was startled when the shrill sound of Coach Rockwell's whistle brought all to attention.

"All right, boys, put on your sweat shirts and take seats over there on the bleachers."

Chip thought to himself, "Doggone, I fell down on the very first real minute of my job. I was supposed to tell Coach Rockwell it was four o'clock." Was it fancy, or did he really detect a grim glare in his direction from the coach? He moved down to the little public address system. At least he'd have that ready if Coach asked for it.

Glancing around with a smile, Rockwell said, "The first thing we've got to do now is get acquainted. Hilton, come here."

"Yes, sir," replied Chip, as he limped to the coach's side.

"Boys, I guess you all know Hilton by this time. However, we'll start just as if we didn't know him. Get one of those big cards, Chip."

Chip soon returned with a large white card.

"All right, good! Now I want you to mark down on this card the nickname of every player on the squad.

We'll start with yours." He spelled out the name. "C-h-i-p, Chip Hilton."

"Yes, sir."

"Okay. Now, let's have last year's letter men," continued the coach. "Morris, I guess everybody knows your nickname—it's been in print enough. Put down 'Speed' for Morris."

Chip rapidly wrote the names which were called out: Chip, Speed, Buzz, and Red. This couldn't be all the letter men there were in school, could it? Then he remembered that last year's team had been a veteran outfit. Only Speed and he had been on the starting five, although Red Schwartz and Buzz Todd had played in a lot of the games. Soapy Smith had been a second-stringer.

Chip's thoughts were interrupted by the coach. "In case you new players don't understand what this is all about, I'll explain. Every player's nickname must be so thoroughly known to the other members of the squad that not a second's time will be lost when it's necessary to attract his attention.

"We always start the season by having a 'name' drill," he continued. "The names you give us now will be used all year and we have to learn them thoroughly. These names will help our teamwork. That right, Buzz?"

"Sure is, Coach!" Buzz Todd nodded his head in agreement.

Rockwell called for the card and read off the names that Chip had written: "*Chip* Hilton, *Speed* Morris,

Taps Browning, *Buzz* Todd, *Red* Schwartz, *Soapy* Smith." Then he went through the list of freshmen: "*Lennie* and *Howie*, the Scott twins, *Mike* Sanders, *Lefty* Peters, *Bill* English," etc.

As the coach read the names from the card, Chip again realized the squad's limitations. Most high schools had seventy or eighty boys trying out the first day of practice, and here was one of the leading teams of the state with only a handful of candidates. . . .

"All right," called Rockwell, "now we'll try the name drill. We'll see if we can learn these nicknames right now. Speed, you, Buzz, Taps, Red, and Soapy go down under the north basket." He flipped the ball to Speed Morris, and the five players dashed down to the end of the floor and stood waiting.

Turning to the rest of the squad, the coach continued, "Now, one of you boys choose four others and take the south basket. English, I mean Bill, suppose you take charge."

Motioning toward the little portable public address set he said, "This thing all right, Chip?"

"Yes, sir," Chip replied, snapping on the electricity and listening anxiously for the familiar hum which signified that the system was warming up.

Coach Rockwell took three quick steps up the bleachers, trailing the long, rubber-covered cord which connected the mike to the instrument box. "Heads up, now," he told them through the mike. "In this practice the player who has the ball—you take the ball up there, Speed—the man who has the ball dribbles, pivots, turns, or stops, but never passes the ball until he hears his name and recognizes the teammate who calls out. Then he passes the ball to that player. If you freshmen will watch Speed's team you'll see what I mean. O.K., Speed, go ahead!"

Speed dribbled hard for the basket, threw a stop with both feet, and then threw a hard overhand pass to Red Schwartz who had screamed, "Speed!" Taps Browning suddenly cut by Red and hollered, "Red!" He received the ball so quickly that he fumbled momentarily. Recovering quickly, he hooked the ball to Soapy Smith who had yelled, "Hey, Taps!" Soon the air was ringing with "Soapy—Taps—Red—Buzz—Speed!"

It was a man-killing practice, and Coach Rockwell knew it. He soon blew his whistle and turned to the freshmen at the other end of the floor.

"All right, Bill, let's go."

This was different. Chip recognized the indecision and lack of confidence immediately. Bill dribbled the ball for ten or fifteen seconds before someone called out—uncertainly. The ball was no longer flying through the air with the zip which had characterized the play of the older players. Suddenly the coach's whistle shrilled and, after one or two passes, the boys came to a halt.

"That's terrible! What's the trouble, Bill?"

"Well, Coach, I guess we don't know the nicknames very well."

"Yes, and what else?" Rockwell asked.

"Well, I guess that's the biggest trouble," Bill answered.

"No, it isn't." Coach Rockwell handed the mike to Chip and leaped down the bleachers. "Let's do a little supposing here. We're playing an important game—a point behind and five seconds to play. There—Speed Morris has the ball. I'm his teammate. I'm under the basket and there isn't an opponent within twenty feet of me. Five seconds to play, remember! I could win the game easily if I could only get the ball—but I'm stuttering around to think of his name—and when I do think of it, I say S-p-e-e-d." The coach's "S-p-e-ed" was almost a whisper; it couldn't be heard ten feet away. "What's wrong with that, Soapy?"

"Same thing that's wrong with Bill's gang, Coach! You ought to holler!" Soapy snapped aggressively.

"All right, you show us. Get up there under the basket and holler. Show these boys how to *holler!*"

Soapy screamed, "S-P-E-E-D! S-P-E-E-D!"

"Louder! Louder!" persisted Rock, and the whole squad laughed as Soapy almost raised the roof screaming "*S-P-E-E-D!*" Speed Morris threw the ball the length of the court almost simultaneously, and Soapy reached up and put the ball in the basket.

"That's how nicknames win ball games," said Coach Rockwell in a satisfied voice as he walked back to the bleachers.

CHAPTER 6

BASKETBALL CALISTHENICS

COACH ROCKWELL sat at his desk laboriously writing a letter. It was not often that the coach wrote his own letters. Usually he tossed his mail to the office secretary and confined his writing to a few scribbled signatures. But this particular letter called for his personal attention, he thought, and when he finished writing, he sat back leisurely in his swivel chair and read it through from beginning to end:

Dear Mrs. Hilton:

Your fears are wholly unnecessary. Chip has applied himself so enthusiastically to his job as manager of the basketball team that I feel sure you need have no further anxiety concerning his happiness.

During my conversation with the boy he expressed disappointment, of course, that his injury prevented him from playing, but at no time did he complain. His chief interest, like most boys, is in sports. I know you understand that. It is perfectly natural and, personally, I feel that the more he can get into basketball the less he will worry about his leg. You may be sure I recognize his mental state. His heart was set on playing basketball this year, and he may yet. At any rate, Doc Jones says the leg might be well enough to enable him to play a little baseball next spring. Both Doc and I will watch him carefully.

You may be sure that your letter will be held in absolute confidence. In fact, I have already destroyed it.

Sincerely,
Henry Rockwell

Coach Rockwell glanced at the office clock. It was three-thirty. He placed the written sheet in the envelope, sealed the envelope tightly, and tossed it into the outgoing mail basket. He glanced thoughtfully around the office and then walked over to the picture of "Big Chip" Hilton which hung on the wall. Looking up at the picture he muttered, "He's a good kid, old-timer." Then he turned and entered the coaching staff's dressing room. In a few minutes he reappeared attired in his gray warm-up suit and hurried off to the gym.

At the sound of Coach Rockwell's whistle the boys moved quickly to the bleachers and put on their sweat shirts. That whistle meant business, and they had all learned that it was unwise to take one more shot or one more dribble. That was one of Rock's pet peeves, and woe to the player who didn't stop immediately when he heard the whistle!

Rockwell glanced along the bleachers at the boys who were sitting there looking at him expectantly. "We're really going to grind this afternoon," he said, "but before we start our regular workout, we'll review a bit. First, there's no room for fancy shooters on this team, and we're not interested in individual color. Just to avoid mistakes, we'll clear up a few things."

He turned to Buzz Todd. "Buzz, s'pose you explain why we have medicine-ball practice every day."

Buzz straightened up. "Medicine-ball practice is what we call our basketball calisthenics. We use a medicine ball to develop and strengthen our fingers and muscles. Then when we change to a basketball—gosh, it's as light as a feather."

"That's right." The coach signaled to Frank Watts for one of the striped medicine balls.

The medicine ball was the exact size of a basketball, but many times heavier. As the coach stood there holding it in both hands, he kept flipping and turning it with the tips of his fingers. Suddenly he threw the heavy ball to Buzz Todd. "All right, Buzz, Taps, Speed, Soapy, and Red—get out here and go through the medicine drill. Don't take off your sweat shirts—only be a second."

The boys leaped to their feet and quickly formed a circle.

"Snap pass!" Coach Rockwell called out. The ball was thrown from one to another from a position between the chest and the waist with a snap of the fingers.

"Up above!" he ordered. Immediately the striped ball was passed back and forth as high above their heads as the boys could reach.

On the command "Downstairs!" the boys spread their feet wide apart and, bending over like football centers, carried the medicine ball far back between the legs. Straightening up quickly they flipped it as hard as they could to a teammate.

"Okay, that's enough," Rockwell cried, and the five players trotted back to the bleachers.

"What's meant by slow motion, Taps?" he asked, looking at the big center whose legs extended over three rows of bleachers. Taps struggled to his feet. "That's movie stuff, Coach, slow like a movie—to develop form."

"All right, show us a one-hand pivot shot—slow motion."

Chip flipped a ball to Taps as he reached the floor and the big fellow dribbled quickly beneath the basket where he gave his impression of a slow-motion pivot shot.

"Notice that Taps has that ball right on the tips of his fingers," broke in the coach just as Taps faked and executed the shot he and Chip had been practicing so consistently. The ball barely touched the backboard and dropped cleanly through the basket.

"Good! That was excellent, Taps," Rockwell said in a pleased manner.

It was easy to understand why Coach Rockwell was concentrating on Taps. The success of the season depended undoubtedly on how Taps handled his height under the defensive as well as the offensive boards. Taps would have to play against one and sometimes two big opponents—taller and heavier. He was still all arms and legs. He had a strong frame, large hands and shoulders, but he hadn't filled out yet.

Taps dribbled back to the bleachers and flipped the ball to Chip with a grin. The look which the two exchanged almost seemed to say "Boy, that old practice is beginning to pay dividends."

Coach Rockwell next singled out Soapy Smith. "What's dummy practice, Soapy?" he asked.

A few chuckles could be heard as Soapy laboriously rose to his feet. "Well—dummy practice, Coach, is playing make-believe."

Everyone grinned as Soapy grew serious and continued belligerently, "I know we always use it when you come back from scouting. Sometimes we dummy-practice two, three days."

Soapy sat down again with a sigh of relief. He was glad *that* was over!

"That's good—far as it goes," said Rock, "but you'll have to do better than that. What else?"

Soapy struggled to his feet again and began uncertainly. "Well, all I know is when you scout a team you always dress up the reserves—" Soapy stopped and looked around with a grin. "That's guys like me." Everyone laughed as he continued, "Then we get numbers like the players we're imitatin'—if he's a dribbler one of us is s'posed to dribble like he does—and if he's a scorer, one of us imitates his shot—"

Soapy was really going strong now and warming up to his subject. "—then you tell us what kind of offense and defense the other team uses," Soapy said, grinning again, "and we dummies practice and play just like the other team does!"

Chet Stewart, who had been standing over at the blackboard on which the coach scribbled plays, snorted and whispered audibly, "Dummies is right!"

"Is that all there is to it?"

"No, sir—no, sir!" Soapy was positive. "After we've got it down pat we play against the varsity and use slow motion and dummy practice to get ready to beat 'em."

Rockwell smiled. "Thanks, Soapy. Now," he continued, "before we go through our repertory of passes, I want to pass out these mimeographed sheets of the give-and-go plays." He handed the sheets of paper to Chip, and soon every boy was scanning the paper carefully.

"We'll practice these plays every night till we master them, but before we do that I want you to study the outlines carefully. Morris and Schwartz are experts with this backcourt maneuver and they'll help you newcomers out with the plays if you'll just ask them. I think the outlines are clear enough, but if they're not, drop in my office any time, and I'll be glad to go over them with you—"

The plays were familiar to Chip. He knew them by heart although his work under the basket had never required that he use them. The plays Rockwell had placed on the sheet were but a few of the many give-and-go

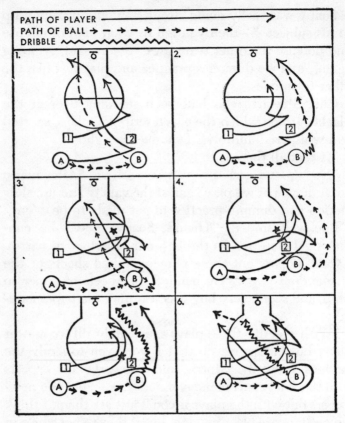

PATH OF PLAYER ——————————→
PATH OF BALL → - → - → - → - → - → - →
DRIBBLE ∿∿∿∿∿∿∿∿∿∿∿∿

plays that Speed and Red had mastered. Coincidentally, Rockwell called for the two backcourt experts just at that moment.

"Speed, you and Red show us the passes we use—slow motion."

Speed and Red hit the floor as soon as the words were

out of Rockwell's mouth, and Chip had to hurry to get the ball to them.

"Let's have the baseball pass, first," Rockwell cried.

Speed carried the ball to a position beside his right ear and assumed much the same stance as a baseball catcher takes when throwing to second base. His elbow extended even with his shoulder, and with exaggerated slowness he brought the forearm forward, turning his shoulder and extending his arm as he followed through by extending his spread fingers along the flight of the ball.

Red caught the ball deftly and repeated the same pass with his left hand.

"Why do we extend the spread fingers along the flight of the ball and then down toward the floor after we've thrown the ball, Buzz?" asked the coach.

"That gives it speed," explained Buzz. "That last little flip puts English on the ball—gives it a lot of zip."

"Yes, but we have to be careful about this 'English,' don't we?" The coach looked at Buzz questioningly.

"Yes, sir," Buzz replied.

"But why?"

"We have to use straight reverse English. Baseball passes are used for long throws, and if we put left-to-right or right-to-left spin on the ball it will curve and maybe cause a fumble," said Buzz.

"That answer is absolutely right! Speed—go down under the south basket. Red, you throw the ball and be careful of that spin."

Speed had reached the basket almost before the coach had finished speaking, and Red threw the ball like a baseball—true and straight—to Speed's waiting hands.

"Roll it back."

Speed used the form and follow-through of a bowler as he sent the ball spinning back to Red. As Red bent over to pick up the ball, Coach Rockwell continued, "Now, Red, throw the ball to Speed with the wrong kind of English."

Red again cocked his arm like a baseball catcher, but this time, at the last moment of release, turned his fingers and wrist clockwise toward the right. The spinning ball started straight enough, but before it reached Speed he was forced to take two or three quick steps away from the basket in order to catch the wildly careening ball.

"Well, I guess that makes it clear enough why you have to use reverse spin on a long pass. That curving ball drew Speed away from the basket and, in a game, might have cost us two points."

Chip observed nodding heads all along the line.

Soon the whole squad was out on the floor and Rock was calling for the passes and drills he wanted. After thirty minutes of action work, the schedule called for shooting practice. This was the part the boys liked best.

After a short, slow-motion rehearsal, the coach called for running lay-up shots. The squad was happy and cheered every successful shot.

Without thinking, Chip had moved out on the court behind the basket and began throwing the loose balls back to the players.

The angry shrill of the whistle brought everything and everyone to a sudden halt. Chip stood holding a ball as Coach Rockwell came clattering down from the "roost" and strode directly toward him.

"What do you think you're doing?" he demanded.

"Why, just throwin' the balls back, Coach," Chip said hesitantly.

"You know my rule about this floor, don't you?"

"Why, sure, Coach, but—"

"No buts! No one's permitted on this floor with street shoes. You get into that storeroom and get a pair of basketball shoes and you wear 'em out here *every day from now on.* I want to see you shootin' a few baskets, too!" A slow smile spread over his lips. "You don't have to shoot baskets with your leg, do you?"

Chip smiled happily. "No, *sir!*"

CHAPTER 7

PICKING THE VARSITY

VALLEY FALLS' basketball hopefuls had looked forward to this particular Saturday morning with eagerness because the town's sports writers and photographers were expected. The dressing room was in an uproar when Chip arrived. Chet Stewart greeted him with a smiling "Good afternoon, Mr. Hilton." The sarcasm did not escape Chip, and he immediately pitched into the work to help out. Chet and Pop were working feverishly to fit each boy with the proper size playing and sweat suits. The assistant managers, Frank Watts and Herb Holden, were scurrying to and from the storeroom with all kinds of equipment.

The satin warm-up suits with their big flowing collars were eagerly desired by all candidates. The Valley Falls colors, scarlet and white, lent themselves admirably to a flashy warm-up suit. In fact, they accentuated the size of everyone. This was a bit of Coach Rockwell's psychology. He made his players look big, one way or another.

The photographers had already set up their cameras out on the court and were talking to Coach Rockwell. As each boy finished dressing he moved down to the south end of the court and joined in passing the ball.

This was no ordinary practice session; it was one of the last steps in selecting the team. Once a player was issued a playing suit and jacket identified with the big number which adorned its front and back, it was difficult to separate that number from his playing identity. Chet had discussed this with Pop and Chip many times, stressing the importance of a number in a boy's basketball career. Most players stuck to one number throughout their playing days. Speed Morris had worn No. 24 ever since he was a freshman.

Looking at the flashily dressed players, Chip felt a deep pang in his heart for the first time in weeks. If things had been different he himself would be wearing a big 26 . . . well, as Rock had said, maybe he wasn't through yet. Anyway, Chet had said Rock wasn't going to give out No. 26 . . . that helped a lot. Maybe he'd be wearing it again . . . before the season was over. . . .

When the cast had been removed from his leg, Doc had said the operation was a success, even though the injured leg was as stiff as a board . . . time would tell. . . .

Chip went through a few manual operations and the brace was firm on his leg. He felt like a million dollars today—he was rarin' to go!

The big clock showed 3:45 P.M. as Chip came out of the dressing room. Coach Rockwell and the photographers were talking near the hall. Taps Browning was standing under one of the side baskets, and Chip joined him.

"Say, Chip," Taps began seriously, "you know that hook shot you showed me before you got hurt?"

"You mean with a step-away?"

"Yes," answered Taps. "Wish you'd help me with it. I could get a lot of points with that." He handed the ball to Chip and waited.

"If my—" Chip caught himself just in time. "It's a good shot, Taps," he said, "and your height makes it hard to stop." He juggled the ball in his hands a couple of times and then turned his back to the basket.

"Look!" Chip half turned his head, shoulders, and hips to the right and faked a shot with his left hand. Almost without pause he then whirled to the left, took a step away from the basket, and following a short leap in the air, transferred the ball to his right hand and dropped it cleanly through the hoop.

"Boy, oh, boy," breathed Taps, "if I could only do that."

Chip had surprised himself. He had pushed off with his injured leg and landed on the floor without the slightest feeling of pain.

He recovered the ball and breathed a sigh of relief. "You'll do it, or I'll know why. Try it slow motion."

For the next fifteen minutes they worked on Chip's pet shots. Taps was coming along fast. "Dunk one, Taps," Chip said. Taps moved back to the free-throw line and then dribbled hard for the basket. Leaping high in the air, he snapped the ball down through the basket without touching the rim.

"*Hey!* Do that again," called a photographer.

Taps grinned at Chip, walked back to the free-throw circle, dribbled hard for the basket and, leaping high in the air, repeated the performance. Taps dunked the ball a half-dozen times and the photographers got several shots of the action. Afterward, each player posed individually with the ball.

When the individual pictures had been taken, Coach Rockwell called all the boys together for a squad picture. Chip had moved up on the bleachers, and his heart jumped when Coach Rockwell called to him, "Come here, Chip—you belong in this picture. Stand over here by me."

"How about Chet and Pop?" Chip asked.

"That's right. Tell 'em to come over."

After the photographers had finished with the players, they asked Coach Rockwell for several individual poses. Chet, Pop, and the boys then really had a chance to see Rock squirm. First, the visitors asked for a picture with a ball; then with a megaphone; and finally one of the coach sitting at a table—supposedly writing the names of the starting "five."

"Chip," called Coach Rockwell when the photographers had completed their work, "go in the gym office and get a couple of rosters and schedules for Mr. Kennedy and Mr. Williams."

Joe Kennedy was sports editor of the *Times*, and Pete Williams was the basketball expert of the *Post*.

"All right, you fellows," called Chet Stewart, "get those suits off and hand them in to Pop. Time's a-wastin'."

Later, Coach Rockwell, Williams, and Kennedy stood near the gym office and watched the practice.

"Isn't that Hilton out there, Rock?" asked Williams, motioning toward Chip, who was shooting baskets with Taps Browning.

"That's him, all right! Bad leg just about broke his heart."

"How is that leg, anyway?" asked Kennedy.

"Takes a long time for an ankle fracture to heal," Rockwell said regretfully. "Sometimes they're never any good for athletics again, you know, and sometimes they turn out stronger than ever."

"He had terrific possibilities," said Kennedy. "He would have been a sure bet for a scholarship anywhere —he and Morris."

"Sure," Coach Rockwell agreed. "State's been after the pair of them since they were freshmen."

"Guess you haven't forgotten Big Chip, have you, Rock?" asked Williams.

"No—never will, I guess! He was the greatest athlete I ever coached! However, this kid, Chip, can do more things. Don't forget he's a couple of years younger than his dad was when he played in high school."

"That's right!" nodded Kennedy.

"Hilton handles himself better than I expected," observed Williams.

"Yes, but he can't do much with that brace. Doc

Jones told me the ankle was as stiff as a board—that's why we're trying to encourage him to work out; loosen it up--we hope!" Coach Rockwell was watching Chip carefully.

"Have to give him credit for trying. Well, good luck, Rock," said Kennedy.

"He'll need it!" Williams remarked as they turned to leave. "So long, Rock."

After Kennedy and Williams had gone, Rockwell called the players to the middle of the court. "Boys," he said, "you don't have to practice any longer today unless you want to. Suit yourselves, however. The gym will be open until you get through. Right, Pop?"

One by one the boys dropped out. This was Saturday and almost every player welcomed the chance to rest. Eventually only Taps and Chip remained.

"I'm sure glad they got the picture of you dunking the ball, Taps."

"Seems to me it's a whole lot like braggin'."

"I wouldn't look at it that way. Heck—not many fellows can do it!"

After a good hour's work they hit the showers and left the gym—Taps heading for home and Chip toward the Sugar Bowl.

CHAPTER 8

THE YOUNG
JOURNALIST

Chip needed help. His thoughts turned to Coach Rockwell, and he decided to pay him a visit. He took the long flight of steps slowly and found the coach seated at his desk with his face buried in a paper. Chip paused at the open door until Rockwell looked up. "Could I see you a minute, Coach?" he asked.

"Sure, Chip. Come in, sit down."

"I'll only be a minute, Coach. I—I'd like to get some advice."

"I've got lots of time. I'm just reading proof on this week's *Yellow Jacket*." Tapping the pages he held in his hand with a pencil, Rock smiled. "See you're getting into print."

"You mean the basketball piece?"

"Yes, Chip, and it's all right, too. Dr. Zimmerman makes me proofread the sports page, you know."

"I can wait, Coach."

"No need; I'm through. This is a fine article, Chip. It's good reading. Not many kids—athletes either, for that matter—know much about the history of basketball."

"I'm glad you like it, Coach. Harry Nichols did most of the work, though."

"Well, anyway, it's good. Now, what's on your mind?"

"That article is just what I want to talk about, Coach. I wrote it originally as a term paper for English, but Taps read it and showed it to Harry Nichols. Nichols asked me to let him print it, and I did. Then I got foolish and agreed to write some more stuff. Now I'm in a jam because I don't know what to write about."

"This story is good, Chip. Of course I'm a little prejudiced, but why don't you write more about basketball?"

"I'd like to, but I've run out of ideas."

"That's easy," said Coach Rockwell. "If you really want to write basketball, go over to the public library. You'll find all the official basketball guides there, from January, 1894, running right up to this year. You'll find records and oddities and all kinds of story material in those little books. They've got all the material you need, all the good stuff."

"That sounds like a *swell* idea."

"By the way," Rockwell added reflectively, "that library won an argument for me several years ago. The high school coaches held their annual meeting here at Valley Falls High a few years ago and several of us got to arguing about the zone. You know, Chip, some coaches feel the zone is the only true defense in basketball—others believe the original philosophy of the game planned defense to be man to man."

"I never thought of that."

"The argument started over the first defense. I said that man to man was the defense Naismith intended when he originated the game. Some sided with me and others said the zone; what an argument!"

"Who was right?"

"You judge. We went to the library and got the first basketball rule book; January, 1894. I can still remember the wording: 'When a player is on the defense he should stick to his man like glue, follow him everywhere, try to prevent him from receiving the ball and, if he should receive it, try to keep him from trying for the goal or passing to a teammate.'"

"Then man to man *was* right!"

"Yes," said Coach Rockwell, nodding his head, "and it's the proper defense to start a player out with today, no matter whether he is going to play on a zone team or not."

"I'll take your word for it, Coach," laughed Chip.

"Since you're thinking about writing sports, Chip, the best thing you can do is to master the philosophy and history of the games you write about. Your problem right now is to get a good basketball background. You'll have to work that out yourself."

"Do you mind if I'm a little late for practice, Coach? After school's about the only chance I have to get to the library."

"Of course not, Chip. You let practice go for this afternoon. I'll tell Chet that I excused you."

"But I—"

"Never mind. School comes first and basketball second. You go to that library."

Right after school Chip made his way to the town's public library. He climbed the long flight of stone steps without stopping. Slowly he made his way into the huge stone building.

The young woman at the information desk directed him upstairs. Golly . . . more steps! As he approached the special reference room he saw a girl standing behind the half-door.

"May I help you?" she asked pleasantly.

"Why, why, yes," faltered Chip, presenting the card the young lady at the information desk had given him. "I'd like to see the basketball guides if I may."

"Certainly. Just a moment." Opening the door she led him to a table. "You sit here and I'll bring the volumes you wish," she said. "What year do you need?"

"May I have the first ones?" asked Chip.

"I can bring you only one at a time. They're very valuable, you know."

"They must be!" Chip looked around at the barred windows and grilled door.

"Don't be so incredulous," the girl said smilingly. "They're rare originals, almost priceless! Just wait a minute and I'll bring you the basketball book."

In a few minutes she returned and Chip gazed down at a thin little volume: *Basketball Guide by James A.*

Naismith—January, 1894. Its leaves were yellow and flaky with age. He buried himself in the old tattered volume. . . .

Chip took a good razzing at the Sugar Bowl Thursday evening. As Speed dropped him in front of the store he was greeted by a chorus, "Hey, gang, look who's here!" "Well, well, Mr. *Yellow Jacket* in person." "Hey, hey, Valley Falls' sports expert." "Now the sports editor said—"

Behind the soda fountain Petey Jackson was reading parts of the article to Ted Williams, Harry Nichols, Red Schwartz, and Biggie Cohen. "Here's Grantland Rice himself," he cried, catching sight of Chip.

"Don't let him needle you, Chip." Ted laughed. "It's darn good!" He waved Chip to a stool beside him in front of the fountain and handed him a copy of the *Yellow Jacket.* "Did you see it?" he asked.

"Yes, I did, Ted. You think it's okay?"

"Mr. Hilton," Harry Nichols interrupted with mock seriousness, "my paper, the *Yellow Jacket,* has authorized me to offer you a weekly contract of five thousand dollars for the exclusive use of your material. Naturally, we expect to feature your stories in our national syndicate."

Chip laughed. "That's not enough—"

"Aw, take the five thousand," advised Red Schwartz.

"I'll take it up with my agent," began Chip.

"Okay, pal," Nichols smiled. Then he added seriously, "No foolin', Chip, it's the best sports article we've printed this year."

Chip made his way back to the storeroom and Speed, Biggie Cohen, and Red Schwartz followed.

The subject of basketball and its history, featured in Chip's *Yellow Jacket* article, was continued.

"Naismith invented the game at Springfield College, didn't he?" asked Red.

"Well, it wasn't exactly Springfield College then," said Chip. "Naismith was teaching at the International Y.M.C.A. Training School, which was located in Springfield, Massachusetts, when he invented the game. It's called Springfield College now, though."

"Is it true," asked Biggie, "that in the beginning it didn't have a name?"

"That's right," agreed Chip.

"How come?" asked Biggie.

"Naismith and one of his students, a guy named Mahon, were talking about a name, and Mahon said, 'Why not call it Naismith Ball?'"

"Why didn't they?"

"Well, Naismith said nobody'd play a game with a name like *that*—"

"Probably right," said Red.

"It was simple enough, though," Chip continued. "Mahon hit the nail right on the head when he said, 'We've got a basket and a ball; why not call it basketball?'"

"Wait till your mother reads the *Yellow Jacket* and finds out how important Mrs. Naismith was in basketball," said Biggie. "She'll be saying Mrs. Naismith helped Dr. Naismith write the rules."

"She *was* important." Chip laughed. "Anyway, she was captain of the first girls' basketball team and one of the first spectators ever to see a game."

"Wonder how she met Naismith?" said Biggie.

"Naismith boarded at her house," said Chip.

"She probably had a crush on him even before the game was invented!" Red chimed in with a laugh.

"She must have been a real sport," said Biggie. "In those days—gosh, girls didn't go in for sports much. Think of it! She was playing basketball way back in 1891!"

CHAPTER 9

WORDS FROM
THE BENCH

THE days seemed to fly. The Christmas holidays came
and went. Chip couldn't find time for half the things
he wanted to do. He was so wrapped up in his sports
writing and basketball that he hardly had time to think.

Today he was late and tried to take the gym steps
two at a time, but the brace restrained him and he was
forced to follow his usual pattern. One, two, three, four
. . . twenty-six. Funny . . . he thought, pausing at his
favorite spot on the broad landing and gazing around
. . . his leg hadn't bothered him a bit up those long
steps. . . .

Continuing into the building, he hurried through the
big trophy foyer and down the long corridor. The hall
was lined with offices on each side—Coach Rockwell's,
Burrell Rogers', Physical Education Instructors'
lounge, and the conference room. Chip called the hall-
way "Bomb Alley." A fellow could always find excite-
ment here.

As he approached the conference room he could hear the laughter of the squad who had assembled for skull practice. There was a lull in the clamor as he opened the door, but as soon as he was recognized he was met by a barrage of greetings: "You're late, kid," "Hiya, Chipso," "Come on in quick—this is good!"

"Hi, gang," Chip tallied, glancing around the big table. He counted noses as he moved to a chair beside Taps. Yes, they were all there. The gang had relaxed again, and he joined the others who were listening to Red Schwartz.

"Yeah, Rock has been giving that pep talk for twenty years," continued Red. He glanced cautiously at the door. Everyone was in good spirits and getting a big kick out of Red. Speed sat beside Red at the head of the big conference table with his back to the door.

"Sure," Red went on, "why, we can always tell when Rock has a banquet coming up. All week he practices his speech on us."

"And are they lous-a-y!" chimed in Speed.

"Lous-a-y is right," grimaced Red.

No one laughed, and in the sudden silence Red and Speed, following the direction of everyone's glance, turned their heads to see Coach Rockwell standing at the door he had quietly opened.

"For Pete's sake," moaned Red. Gazing at Speed as if looking for help he managed another "Pete's sake!"

Coach Rockwell smiled and raised an eyebrow in Red's direction. Walking to the head of the table his glance shifted rapidly from face to face as he greeted the squad with his usual "All right, boys, let's go!"

"All present and accounted for, Coach," Chip reported.

"—And everybody on time but me," quipped the coach. "Boys," he went on, "this afternoon I've really got time to say some of the things I should have brought to your attention the first day of practice.

"Morale is an important factor in athletics. All the things I'm going to talk about today center around that important factor. Morale means team spirit; means enthusiastic practices, fighting for the team and the school whether you're on the bench or on the floor.

"Courage is an important thing in life and in athletics. It takes courage to study when you're tired just as much as it does to fight out there on the court when the going gets tough. Often a game gets more important to a player than school—that's bad. School's first. Basketball's second. Furthermore, the disaster which ineligibility can bring to a team can't be overemphasized. Certainly it's much better to have a poor player and be able to use him for the entire season than to have a star half a year and then, because of ineligibility, lose him after he's become important to the team.

"All of you are capable of passing your subjects. Half the battle in school is being regular in attendance and keeping up with your home assignments—"

"We sure get plenty of homework," murmured Red.

"Most of you know how I feel about 'outside' ball playing. Sooner or later you'll meet a thirty-cent promoter who will want to cash in on your publicity. Fly-by-night leeches like to capitalize on players whose names are on the sports pages."

Coach Rockwell's jaws squared as he bit off his words. "You can't play outside ball and play for Valley Falls High, too! You devote your playing to Valley Falls High exclusively or you turn in your uniform! Is that clear?

"So much for outside ball. And let's skip strategy for the moment. Plays aren't everything. A team to be successful must have something more. First, a fierce desire to win; second, the will to persevere in practice; and third, team spirit and teamwork—confidence in one another—

"Chip, do you remember the play that won the Section championship for us two years ago in the final game against Parkton?"

"I sure do, Coach!"

"Well," prompted Rockwell, "go ahead! Tell us what happened!"

"There were only five minutes to go and we were six points behind, and Tim Murphy took time out. You sent word for us to feed Sy Barrett—and we did! Sy was hot! He hit three quick sets while Parkton was scoring only one point, and then, with just a few seconds to go, Sy took a set from his favorite spot near the left side line. We were one point behind with ten seconds to go when he took the shot—but he missed!"

Chip nodded his head toward Speed. "Speed drove in for the rebound and got the ball. He really could have tried a follow-in shot—but he didn't! He surprised everybody when he hooked the ball right back to Sy—

Parkton's players had all rushed back under the basket to get the rebound, and there wasn't *anyone* near Sy. He took aim, just as though he were practicing, and let the ball fly. Right after he shot, the gun sounded, but the ball was in the air and swished through the basket just as though it had eyes—and we won by a point!"

"That was s-o-m-e shot!" marveled Speed. "You know, Coach, I didn't have the least doubt that Sy would sink it."

"Me either!" chimed in Chip. "Old Sy might miss one—but he'd never miss *two* from the same spot."

Coach Rockwell nodded his head reflectively. "You're right," he agreed. "What I'm trying to bring out here is the fact that Speed and Chip here, and the rest of the boys, had enough confidence in Barrett to place the responsibility of winning that game solely on Sy's shoulders."

"Don't see how he could be a better set shot than Buzz," ventured Taps.

"Get out!" remonstrated Buzz in a self-conscious manner. "Gosh—Sy was the best set-shot man that ever lived!"

"Well, I never saw him play," said Taps, "but I'd bet on you!"

"That brings us to practice," broke in the coach.

Everyone leaned a little closer as he went on. "Practice is vital! *Repetition is the secret of all knowledge!* Lots of high school stars reach the top too soon and feel they don't need to practice. Newspaper headlines often result in enlargement of the occipital bones—

commonly known as swelled head—and when that happens to a player, he has reached his limit. I prefer average basketball players who can be improved. We have no time here for swell-headed players, for we all realize we have weaknesses which practice alone can remedy."

Chip had been so engrossed in the meeting that he had forgotten the time. Now he glanced at his wrist watch . . . it was 4:35. He attracted Coach Rockwell's attention and tapped his wrist watch significantly.

"All right," nodded the coach, "time is short, but before we break up I'd like to refer to the rules. Valley Falls plays according to the book and uses no fancy blocks or tricks. I've no time for players who resort to arm pulling, pushing, and holding. We play clean! Furthermore, there's only one man on the floor who can talk to the officials—that's the captain! Any player who speaks disrespectfully to the referee or umpire comes out of the game—immediately—win or lose. And that brings up another important matter, the captain. We'll elect him in the dressing room just before the Alumni game!"

CHAPTER 10

REPETITION PAYS

CHIP HILTON got up from his seat and tiptoed to Professor "Maggots" Magnus' desk and dropped his history examination paper on top of the rest. It was his last term exam and he had the feeling that he had hit it for a bull's-eye.

Outside, the cool crisp air made his blood jump. He was anxious to get to the gym. Maybe Chet or Pop would shoot baskets with him. Coach Rockwell had been driving the team hard; moving, demonstrating, explaining, and forcing them to rehearse a play or a game situation again and again. Chip thought of Coach Rockwell's pet phrase: "Repetition is the secret of all knowledge!" Well, this team ought to be smart enough . . . they repeated everything they did about fifty times!

He dressed quickly and clumped up the stairs. Soon the gym was full of boys working on individual skills. Chip moved over to a practice basket and sat down on the floor with his feet just touching the free-throw line. From this awkward position he used only his arms, wrists, and fingers to speed the ball with almost effortless ease into the basket. His accuracy was amazing, and several of the freshman players gathered around and watched him with admiration. Taps trotted over under the basket. Chip was using the overhand spin shot, and Taps, standing directly under the ring, stretched his long arms above his head and caught the ball just as it dropped through the net.

Speed came dashing over dribbling a ball. "Move over, Dead Eye!" he said. He dropped down beside Chip. "How's about a little competition for cokes?" he challenged.

"Okay, sucker." Chip grinned. "Taps, you keep count. Best out of ten."

Red Schwartz came dribbling around under the basket and back to Chip's other side. "Can I get in it?" he asked.

"Huh, fresh fish," grunted Speed, poking Chip with his elbow.

"All right, who's first?" interrupted Taps.

"Aw, let the big shot shoot first," someone said.

"You mean me, I presume?" Red said, bowing politely.

"Right the first time!" was the retort.

Red missed the first three shots amid raucous jeers and jibes, but finally hit a streak and ended up with five out of ten.

"True to form," snorted Buzz, "fifty-fifty, that's good old Red."

"Good enough to take you!" retorted Red.

Speed was next and managed to cage seven of his ten shots. All eyes were on Chip now. He missed the first shot and then ripped the cords for nine straight.

"Nice going, Chip," Taps beamed, snapping the ball back to him gleefully. "Go on, see how many you can hit!"

"Lucky stiff!" Speed said morosely as he sprang to his feet.

Chip continued and, after shaky tenth and eleventh shots, ran his string to sixteen straight before missing.

Chet Stewart had joined the group. "Nice shooting, Chip," he said. "Too bad some of the All-Americans can't shoot like that!" He glanced meaningly at Speed, Red, Taps, and Buzz. Then, shaking his head mournfully, he walked away.

Chip limped over to the bleachers and sat down by Frank Watts. Glancing back at the group he saw that Speed, Taps, Red, and Buzz were standing shoulder to shoulder on the fifteen-foot line, shooting fouls in turn while Soapy retrieved the ball. From their determined faces and manner he knew that Chet's pointed remark had struck home.

"Wish they could all shoot fouls like Buzz," Frank said earnestly. "If they could, Valley Falls wouldn't lose many games this year. Coach says about ninety per cent of all games between good teams are won on free throws."

"He's sure right," agreed Chip, nodding his head in agreement. "Buzz hit forty-two straight the other afternoon; of course, that was just practice."

Glancing at the big gym clock he saw that there were still ten minutes before regular practice began. What a difference a few weeks can make, he thought. The workouts had been tough, and Coach had lived up to his reputation as a slave driver, but the gang had loved every minute of it—even when they were griping. . . . Coach sure knew the secret of coaching . . . "Keep them busy, make it short, and have fun!"

Yes . . . four of the first five were set. Speed was at left forward and a cinch to be elected captain before the first game . . . Taps was improving every day. He felt a sense of satisfaction in that . . . he had worked with Taps every afternoon . . . sometimes for a solid hour. Funny, how well he was getting around on his bad leg. . . .

Red Schwartz and Buzz Todd were sure of the guard positions . . . good old Red—happy-go-lucky spark plug and a great backcourt player, with plenty of drive . . . and last but not least, Buzz, the best shot on the squad . . . Buzz could sink them from any place on the court. When Buzz concentrated on a shot and got set— just rack up two points, that's all—two points. . . .

The fifth spot was wide open but Chip had already tabbed little Mike Sanders as his choice. Mike and Lefty Peters were fighting tooth and nail to make the last starting berth. It didn't matter much who won out . . . both were good!

Jeepers! The first game was less than two weeks away . . . seemed only yesterday was the first day of prac tice. . . .

Frank Watts elbowed his shoulder. "Time, Chip," he said, nodding his head in the direction of the clock.

Chip turned and glanced up at the "roost," but Coach Rockwell had already started down from his perch and waved his hand to show that he knew the time. The sharp blast of the whistle halted all activity on the court, and the gang trotted over to the bleachers.

Rockwell pulled the portable blackboard in front of the seated players and busied himself with chalk and eraser.

"Boys," he said, "in another ten days we'll be on our way. There's a lot more to basketball than offense and defense—psychology and strategy are favorite weapons of champions! I'd like to give you one of the strategy weapons that a lot of teams use effectively—the 'press!'" He turned back to the blackboard and expertly drew a number of diagrams and lines on the black surface.

Rockwell was expert in the use of chalk and blackboard or pencil and paper. The replica of a court which he drew on the board was almost perfect.

"The defensive players, in this case the squares—1, 2, 3, 4, and 5—have just scored, and their opponents have taken the ball out of bounds under the basket. Instead of retreating beyond the ten-second line and waiting for the team which has just been scored upon to advance the ball across the ten-second line—the scoring players have pressed close to their opponents and are guarding them all over the court—

"This *team* strategy means that the burden of ad-

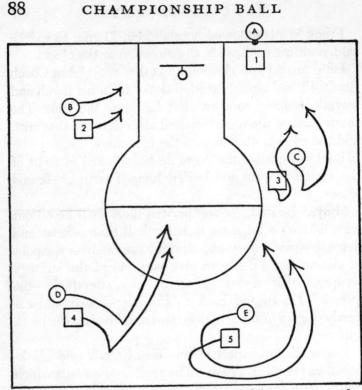

vancing the ball across the ten-second line is upon the team which has just been scored upon. A bad pass, or the use of more than ten seconds in advancing the ball across the center of the court, will result in possession of the ball by the forcing players—1, 2, 3, 4, and 5.

"In the losing minutes of a game, when a team is behind in the score, this strategy is imperative. Such forcing may result in possession, or an intercepted pass—and an easy score."

Rockwell paused and searched the eyes of the intense group of boys. What he saw must have pleased him, for there was satisfaction in his voice as he continued:

"However, pressing calls for the utmost in team play. Each player must concentrate on his immediate opponent and stick with him—no matter where he goes. The emphasis here is on playing each opponent closely and forcing an error. It pays off well if well played.

"Think it over, boys. We'll probably have to use the 'press' many times before this season is over. Next week, we'll work it out in practice—today, we'll stick to our fundamentals."

It was a tired squad, two hours later, that welcomed Rockwell's "Hit the showers!" But long after the noisy crowd had left the gym, Taps and Chip worked on their shots and under-the-basket tricks. If repetition was the price—they were sure willing to pay it!

CHAPTER 11

FIRST BLOOD

THE long-awaited Wednesday and the season's first real scrimmage arrived at last. The big scoreboard was all set. It had been readied for the first time since practice had started five weeks ago. Old Pop was pressing buttons and checking the corresponding lights on the board.

Down at the south basket tall, agile players were dashing around and practicing all kinds of shots. These players made up the Flying Aces, one of the best professional teams in the country. Representing the big airplane company which was located a few miles outside of Valley Falls, they were finishing up their training for the opening of the professional basketball league, and Coach Rockwell had asked them up for a practice game.

One of Valley Falls High's great players of former years was with them—Arch Thomas. Six feet, eight inches in height and weighing two hundred and forty pounds, Arch had been an All-American at State after his graduation from Valley Falls High School. Now he was the professional league's outstanding center.

Chip was sitting midway up the bleachers with Frank Watts and Herb Holden.

"Look at the size of them." Frank grimaced admiringly. "They make us look like a grade school team."

"And how!" agreed Herb. "They're all good shots too."

Chip was excited. "Guess Coach wants to *really* find out how good we are!"

Just then Arch Thomas left his teammates and three pairs of admiring eyes watched him leap lightly up the bleachers, three at a time, until he reached Coach Rockwell's side. There Coach Rockwell and he engaged in earnest conversation. From time to time they gestured toward Taps Browning who was moving about under the north basket, tapping up rebounds, and occasionally trying his pivot shot.

"Must outweigh Taps more'n fifty pounds," Herb began, voicing Chip's thoughts, "and he's at least four inches—"

"Can't be," interrupted Chip. "Taps is six-six!"

"Looks like he'd make two of him, anyway," said Frank, "but the bigger they are, the harder they fall!"

"Yes, if they don't fall on *you!*" retorted Herb.

The official's whistle ended all activity on the floor. Just like Rock, Chip was thinking . . . everything had to be just so . . . scoreboard had to be rigged up and everything run just like a regular game . . . including two officials. Hope the gang makes a good showing . . . won't have to worry about Speed and Buzz and

Red . . . but this isn't three-man basketball. As the coach had said in that first meeting, "Today's basketball can't be played with five men—you need ten or twelve first-stringers!"

Chip wore no gym suit today . . . but maybe he could work out later. . . .

Coach Rockwell and the visiting coach were talking with the two officials in the center of the floor. As they left the court the referee's whistle served notice that it was time to start the scrimmage.

The Flying Aces lined up quickly and confidently. Arch Thomas took a position outside the center ring, facing the south basket, and began talking to the referee who was holding the ball.

Valley Falls' Big Reds surrounded Coach Rockwell who was giving last-minute instructions. Chip moved over close. He was curious about that fifth starter . . . would it be Mike, Lefty, or Soapy?

Coach Rockwell was speaking. "Speed, you act as captain; Red and Buzz at the guards; Taps at center." Then clearing his throat, he looked at little Mike Sanders and clapped him softly on the shoulder. "You go in at the other forward, Mike."

He extended his right hand, and the five starters placed their hands on his as he continued, "We'll play this practice game just like we play a regular game—for keeps! Let's go!"

The team dashed out on the floor with shouts of encouragement from the bench: "Let's go, gang!" "Pour it on 'em!" "Whaddaya say, gang? Whaddaya say!"

The ball was tossed in the air and the scrimmage was on. Big Arch Thomas had leaped forward and up with the whistle, and the resulting contact completely spoiled Taps' jump. Before Browning even regained his balance, Thomas had cut by him and, receiving a return pass from No. 10, had dribbled to the right of the south basket. As Buzz switched to cover him, Thomas bounce-passed to the little Ace forward, No. 8, who deftly dropped the ball in the basket for the first score.

The first half was dominated by the Aces. Their superior height and weight precluded any effective Valley Falls play under either basket. Taps was buffeted right and left, and it was only through the set-shot efforts of Red and Buzz that Valley Falls scored at all.

Lefty Peters took Mike's place for the last six minutes of the half and looked good—making two baskets on quick-break plays with Speed and Red.

Speed kept the defense from falling apart by daring interceptions, but at the end of the first half the scoreboard showed: Visitors 36—Valley Falls 19.

"Are they good!" whispered Frank, moving close to Chip's side as they followed Chet Stewart and the team into the dressing room.

"How you goin' to play clean against those guys?" demanded little Mike pugnaciously, glaring around the room at the discouraged faces of his teammates. "They grab your arms and shove—"

"Shut up!" bellowed Chet Stewart menacingly from his position by the door. "Sit down and keep quiet! No one talks in here 'cept the coach!"

When Coach Rockwell entered the room a few seconds later, the only sound was the slap-clip, slap-clip of old Pop's nimble fingers as he doused Speed's legs with his precious rubbing lotion and worked away loosening up the muscles.

Chip got set for the explosion . . . this should be good . . . they had it coming. . . . He laid the scorebook on the table and moved away.

"All right," Coach Rockwell began, studying some scribbled notes on a small card, "all right now—we haven't much time to talk nor much to talk about." Then, looking at Speed, he startled everyone as he exploded, "A fine captain! They run your team into the ground and no time-outs—no change of defense—no holding the ball on offense! Nothing!"

Without waiting for an answer he pointed an accusing finger at Browning and his words clicked like a typewriter. "Taps. Taps! TAPS! How'd you ever get that name? You haven't even seen the ball, much less tapped it! Taps? Huh!" His voice was scornful and bitter as he continued, "You're so scared of Thomas you'd jump over the basket if he said boo!"

For a long minute there wasn't a sound in the room. Chip was all confused. For Pete's sake. . . . Speed had been playing his head off and Taps . . . why, Taps had been boxed by two and sometimes three of the Aces every time he got near the basket. . . . What did Rock expect?

"If I have to run this team from the bench, I'll do it! Now pay attention!" Moving to the strategy board, a small-sized replica of the playing court, which Stewart had set up on the rubbing table, he placed the chessmen in a two-one-two zone formation.

"We'll try the two-one-two zone. Why, Red?"

"That'll do it, Coach," Schwartz nodded eagerly, "I was thinking about that a minute ago. The zone will block those big guys away from the basket."

"What do you think, Speed?" Coach Rockwell looked at Morris intently as he waited.

"It's the ticket, Coach. I must have been asleep—but I thought you'd tell me if you wanted me to make any changes."

"On the floor, the captain's the boss," said Rockwell. "It takes brains to win games and a smart, thinking captain doesn't wait for a letter from the coach before making a decision. I told you to act as captain—and I expect action! Right?"

Speed nodded as Coach Rockwell shifted the chessmen to the other end of the strategy board and continued, "On the offense we'll quick-break every time— every time, you hear—and if we can't beat them down with the break, we'll set up the horseshoe and draw those big, slow fellows out from under the basket and then outrun 'em. Understand, Browning?"

"Yes, Coach," Taps chopped through set jaws. "I guess I was foolish to try to score from underneath against all that height. They stopped every shot I tried!"

"All right—we'll start the same five—and don't forget—they have a big lead and that means we've *got* to get that ball. Let's go!"

The second half was different. Either the change of tactics and the continuous pressure which the youngsters kept on the Aces were getting results, or the pros had tired and were coasting; Chip couldn't tell which. At any rate, Buzz and Red were hitting from outside and Speed and Mike were cutting around Taps for basket after basket. After eight minutes of play the score stood: Aces 42—Valley Falls 34. The pros called time out and went into a huddle.

Coach Rockwell substituted Lefty Peters for Mike Sanders and the game continued. It was just the same except that now Taps was setting up a post at the free-throw line and, after feeding Speed and Lefty as they cut by, was pivoting around Thomas and getting an inside position on the big center under the basket. With six minutes left to play he scored three quick follow-up baskets and the score stood: Aces 54—Valley Falls 51. The pros again called time.

Coach Rockwell then sent Soapy Smith, the two Scott boys, Lefty Peters, and Bill English in to finish out the game. The Aces seized the opportunity to put on a freeze, passing the ball from one to the other without tying to shoot, and the scrimmage ended without further scoring. Final score: Aces 54—Valley Falls 51.

As the players left the floor, Arch Thomas and Coach Rockwell sat down together on the home bench.

"What do you think, Arch?" asked Rockwell.

"First five look good, Coach," the big center said earnestly, "but the subs are plenty weak."

"Yes, that's the score."

Arch Thomas shook his head soberly. "Looks like a tough row ahead, Coach."

Coach Rockwell seemed lost in thought but finally remarked, "Doesn't seem possible Alumni game's only a week away. Be with us?"

"Sure will! Couldn't keep me away!"

"What about Browning, Arch? Think he's got what it takes?"

"Yes, I do."

"He didn't look very good that *first* half."

Thomas grinned. "Well, you said to pour it on him. And that's what we did! He took everything we gave him that first half without much of an argument, but he was sure different in the second half."

"Browning is Chip Hilton's protégé. Chip's been working with him by the hour."

"Too bad you don't have Hilton this year, Coach. He's about the best high school player I ever saw!"

"He's that, all right! But you know, Arch, that Browning kid has great possibilities. All he needs is a little confidence."

"Well, I can take care of that, Coach. I'll see he gets some—in the Alumni game!"

CHAPTER 12

THE ALUMNI GAME

THE Alumni Game did not count in the season's record, but it was important to everyone: important to Coach Rockwell's coaching because it gave his team game practice; to the student body because they could get a pre-season view of the team and enjoy the dance that followed the game; to the Alumni because they could meet old friends and see the "kids."

Chip had been as busy as Pop Brown. He had gotten the roll of tickets, the ticket-seller's change, the money box, and had seen that the box office and the gate attendants were all set. He had worried about this part of the manager's job for it was his responsibility to see that the money and tickets were turned over to Burrell Rogers.

Later he had helped Pop and Chet in the dressing room, had checked the big scoreboard, helped get the Alumni players equipped, and now he was seated at the scorer's table, hands under his chin, elbows resting on

Valley Falls' brand-new scorebook. In a few minutes the Big Reds would open their new basketball season.

It was a tradition at Valley Falls that the captain of the Big Reds for the coming basketball season would be elected just before the first game. That was the reason Coach Rockwell and Chet Stewart were not in the dressing room with the team. Coach Rockwell always sat with the Alumni and coached the old-timers. The newly elected captain was supposed to take charge of the varsity.

Chip was watching the hall leading to the Valley Falls dressing room. There was no question in his mind as to who would be this year's basketball captain . . . but you never could tell. . . . Gosh, if he were in that dressing room right now . . . maybe there would be a scramble between him and Speed for the post . . . Speed and he had been co-captains of the football team. . . . They might even have been elected co-captains of the basketball team . . . that would have been something! Co-captains in two sports. . . .

Coach Rockwell always delegated Pop to stay with the team before the first game and to pass out the little slips of paper. He could still remember last year when they had elected Butch Regan. . . . It wouldn't be long now! . . .

He shifted his eyes as a round of applause greeted the entrance of Arch Thomas and the old-timers. Arch dribbled the ball down to the south basket. Then there was a quietness which always preceded the entrance of the Big Reds. Every eye was on the doorway through which a new captain would lead the Valley Falls hopefuls.

Suddenly a tremendous cheer hit the ceiling as Speed Morris, head down and dribbling the ball a mile a minute, dashed out the door and headed for the north basket. No doubt about who was the leader of this team!

The Big Reds were full of pep; their red-and-white-clad figures dashed under the basket and back up the floor so fast that it was hard to follow the ball—they were rarin' to go!

With the shrill of the official's whistle, the players began to take off their sweat suits. Rock was talking to Arch Thomas, Butch Regan, and the rest of the starting Alumni five. Speed was standing in front of the varsity bench where he was soon joined by Red Schwartz, Taps Browning, Buzz Todd, and little Mike Sanders. The tension was terrific.

Chip hadn't expected to feel this way; but his whole being was filled with that numb, trancelike, pre-game hypnosis which all athletes feel just before the kickoff in football, the first pitch in baseball; the center jump in basketball. There was a sinking sensation in the pit of his stomach, and something was pounding at his chest. He could hardly breathe. Then the referee tossed the ball into the air, and it was all forgotten: the game was on!

Arch Thomas outjumped Taps and drove hard for the basket just as he had done in the practice game. This time, however, Taps swung about almost in mid-air and was right behind Thomas, his hands waving

Chip's chest swelled with pride . . . Taps was fighting. . . .

Taps had jumped too quickly, but Chip was sure the buck fever had ended after that first jump. The old-timers had begun to move the ball here and there, trying to find an opening—then the ball was passed to Thomas, who feinted Taps out of position, pivoted, and scored. Alumni led by two points!

Chip watched Speed and Red. There was a sureness in their play which was not evident in the running and passing of Buzz and little Mike Sanders. Speed and Red were completely relaxed, but there was a noticeable change of pace when they were forced to team up with one of the others.

Taps Browning was standing on the free-throw line, back to the basket, feeding his teammates with the same passes he had practiced so faithfully in Chet Stewart's wall drill. Red Schwartz scored the first Valley Falls basket on a beautiful back-bounce pass. The score was tied at two all.

Chip was thinking about Taps. This would probably be the best test he would have all year . . . Arch Thomas was undoubtedly far superior to any high school player Taps would face. So far as that was concerned, thought Chip, Thomas was probably the best center Taps would *ever* face.

Toward the end of the first half, the play of the Alumni slowed down noticeably. Condition was beginning to tell. The half ended with the score 26—22 in favor of the Alumni.

The second half was no contest. Speed and Red scored almost at will, and Chip was so busy with his scorebook he hardly saw the game as the varsity ran up the score to win, 66—45. The first victory of the season!

The Valley Falls gym could seat three thousand spectators. It had been filled to capacity on this first night and now, as the crowd started home, all but two persons were talking about Valley Falls' basketball team.

Stinky Ferris wanted to talk about the game, but Joel Ohlsen was in a sullen mood and stalked along silently. When they arrived at their corner, Stinky said, "Going straight home or going down to Mike's?"

"I'm not going down to Mike's. Wish I'd never gone there."

"What's the matter, Joel?"

"I'm in trouble."

"What kind of trouble?"

"Oh, I got in a mess down at the poolroom."

"What doin'?"

"I got into a dice game," Fats said miserably.

"At the Academy?"

"No, after the Academy closed up, I went with some fellows to play cards and then we got into a dice game."

"What happened?" Stinky persisted.

"I lost a lot of money—more money than I ever had in all my life."

"Well, if you didn't have the money, how could you lose it?"

"I gave them a couple of checks."

"So what? Pay them and don't play with them any more."

"But I haven't got the money, Stinky," Joel said desperately. "Don't you understand? I don't even have an account in the bank—I lost nearly a thousand dollars."

"A thousand *dollars?*"

"Yes, and I don't know where I'm going to get it."

"You mean you wrote some checks and you don't even have a bank account?" Stinky gasped.

"That's right!"

"But—but—that's criminal, isn't it? Why'd you ever do it?"

"Why'd I do it? Why does anyone do things like that? I only had a few dollars and I lost that, and then I borrowed some money and I lost that. So I wrote the checks figuring I'd win 'em back."

"What are you going to do?"

"I don't know. I gave them my driver's license and everything else."

"What if they put the checks in the bank?"

"They said they'd hold them—till I could get the money—but I don't know where in the world I could get a thousand dollars!"

"Who were they?" asked Stinky.

"That Smitty-something and a guy called Red. I don't even know their last names."

"Didn't you write their names on the checks?"

"No, I made 'em out to cash. What am I going to do, Stinky?"

Later, as Stinky walked down the dark street which

led to the flats, he was thinking desperately of some way to help his friend. Stinky had often daydreamed of the time when Joel Ohlsen would need him and he'd be able to show his loyalty. Well, here it was—and he couldn't do a thing.

A thousand dollars was a lot of money. It was more than Stinky had ever seen. A thousand dollars would take care of his folks for a whole year. It wasn't right; Joel had been tricked out of the money. But if Mr. Ohlsen ever heard about this it would be just too bad!

CHAPTER 13

FREEZE THE BALL

IT WAS a sober group of youngsters who were gathered around the radio in the Hilton living room a week later. Stan Gomez, WTKO's sportscaster, was summarizing the high school basketball games of the past week.

"Yes—Weston, last year's champs, are continuing their winning ways. Looks as if they're the team to beat for the championship. Yep, the same five boys who walked off the court up at the University last March with the big trophy walked away with their third straight victory of the current season Wednesday night at Parkton, 44 to 39. That's the thirty-fourth consecutive win for the Cardinals.

"And last year's great runner-up team, the Stratford Indians, chuck-full of veterans, seems to be heading straight for this year's finals. Yep!—the Indians scalped the Salem Sailors, 52 to 21.

"Down at Valley Falls, the Big Reds got off to a bad start—losing to Batson's zone defense, 44 to 35. Batson's zone defense completely dominated the game. Coach

Henry Rockwell has only three holdovers from last year's regulars which may account for the home-court defeat. That Batson zone makes most of them look bad though—veterans or otherwise.

"Over at Steeltown, the story was different. The Iron Men won two games this past week and ran their string to four in a row. Steeltown got off to an early start this year. Looks like they'll be one of the strong teams of the state. Over at Dane—"

Speed reached up and turned off the radio. He was downcast. "How's your ankle, Taps?" he asked.

"No good." Taps stood up, tried a step or two, and then limped over to the couch and sat down dejectedly.

"How'd it happen?" Speed was puzzled.

"Just turned it—that's all."

"Don't see how you could. Never knew anyone else to turn an ankle after Pop taped it."

"Coach see it?" asked Red.

"Not till after the game."

"Hope it's okay for the Parkton game," said Red.

"It will be!" Taps was determined.

"We might have won the Batson game, anyway," Red said, "if Coach hadn't taken Mike out."

"Coach couldn't leave Mike in," Chip broke in. "You know that! Coach isn't going to let anybody talk to the officials except Speed here. Mike's been told that half-a-dozen times!"

"I know, Chip," said Speed, "but Mike's been having a lot of trouble, and he's all upset. You know what else he's doing!"

"Let's skip that!" suggested Chip.

"Live and learn," said Red, shrugging his shoulders.

"Live and lose, you mean," said Speed.

Red changed the subject. "Coach sure hates that Batson zone," he said.

"Yes, but we shoulda knocked them off, Red," Speed said.

"But Rock *said* it was his fault we lost."

"Look, Red," Speed shook his head. "You know it wasn't Rock's fault as well as I do. We never lost to Batson here at home before, and they've always used a zone. Heck, we just didn't have it!"

"Well, anyway," said Chip, "Coach is having the lines changed to make a bigger court. He's gonna have two ten-second lines—one for each team. That'll make the front court 'bout twice as large."

"Nothin' went right in that game, anyway," said Red. "Buzz couldn't hit, and neither Mike nor Lefty did us any good."

"Right!" Speed nodded. "We never did get organized. Well, I gotta go home. Goin', Red?"

As soon as the door closed Chip turned to Taps. "Now give me the low-down, Taps. What's the real score?"

"Well, Chip, Pop didn't tape my ankle the other night. It was my fault. Guess I was too excited to ask him, and after I turned it—I didn't want to tell Coach 'cause I knew Pop'd be in a jam."

Chip nodded his head. "That's just what I figured. But Chet Stewart's just as much responsible for checking the ankles as Pop." He stopped suddenly. "Hey! So am I! Gosh, I never thought of that!"

"It wasn't anyone's fault but *mine*," Taps said firmly. "I was one of the first dressed, but everyone was so busy and so rushed I thought I'd let it go just that one time."

"*One* time—" Chip was thoroughly aroused now. "Gosh, we've got to get that thing attended to right away. I'll call Doc Jones! What's his number? Wait, I've got it!"

He dialed the number and stood waiting impatiently until the receiver clicked at his ear. "Hello—Doc? This is Chip Hilton. Yes! Doc, I hate to call you this time of night, but I wonder if you could do me a favor and come over to look at Taps' ankle—yes, Taps Browning! Yes, he turned it the other night in the Batson game. You will? Thanks!" Chip hung up the receiver. "He's coming right over, Taps. Hope he can fix it up for the Parkton game; whole season just about depends on you!"

In the days which followed, Taps' ankle improved a little, but he was still limping when the Big Reds lined up for the Parkton game. Fortunately, Coach Robbins had realized that his inexperienced players couldn't keep pace with Valley Falls in scoring, and he had instructed them to hold the ball on the offense. He had figured that a passing and stalling style might upset the classier Valley Falls team, and this was just exactly what was happening.

Lefty Peters, Buzz Todd, and Taps couldn't take it. They were lunging at the ball trying to intercept passes, and providing a perfect reaction to Coach Robbins' planned strategy.

As soon as Speed realized Parkton's objective, he called for a time-out. In the huddle he laid down the law. "You fellows have to play a careful game," he said. "This bunch isn't going to run with us. We're playing right into their hands. We're going to hold that ball, too. Now don't forget—Lefty, Buzz, Taps—don't make bad passes. They can't beat us as long as we have the ball. Move it around and let Red and me take the chances. Understand?"

Parkton continued its stalling tactics throughout the first and second periods. Their strategy was working and at the end of the half they were leading, 9—7.

Up in the stands the fans were talking excitedly. Basketball like this was played twenty years ago. In those days teams in the lead, when opposing a zone defense, often sat down on the floor and made no further attempt to score.

"Why, in those days," someone was saying, "Valley Falls often beat Parkton and Batson by scores of five to two; sometimes two to one. I remember one game in which the score was one to nothing!"

At the end of the first half the boys filed into the dressing room without a word. Coach Rockwell studied the scorebook and then turned his attention to the shot sheets. Herb Holden and Frank Watts were responsible for these charts. Coach Rockwell considered the information they contained extremely valuable.

The shot sheets were printed replicas of a basketball

court in scale. The number of every player who attempted a goal was jotted down on the shot sheet as close as possible to the exact spot from which the shot was taken. If the shot was successful, the player's number was circled.

Herb Holden's job went even further. He was supposed to list all assists which led to a score, the number of rebounds which a player secured from his own backboard, and the number of times each player recovered the ball from the opponent's board. Loss of the ball because of bad passes, interceptions, and dribbling was included.

In the hall outside Coach Rockwell's office a big chart was posted which listed each player and his performance for all games to date. After each game, the information contained on the game charts was transferred to Coach Rockwell's "player performance chart." Anyone could look at this chart and tell almost at a glance what players were important in the games which had been played so far.

Coach Rockwell stepped over in front of the two rows of benches; the players were all attention. Even though they were behind in the score they could sense that Rock was satisfied with their play during the half.

"Boys," he began, "this is a game which can be easily lost. We've got to be careful. I wasn't surprised that you were a bit upset at first, but you are playing well now. When Speed took that time-out and told you just what Parkton was trying to do, I wondered if you could pull yourselves together and play smart. Bill Robbins is a clever coach. I had dinner with him, and he never said a thing about pulling this little surprise. Just what is their strategy, Red?"

"It's just like Speed said in the huddle, Coach. He said they were freezing the ball and trying to get us so upset we'd lose our heads. Speed told us not to try to force a score but to pass the ball around until we got a good shot."

"That's right, Red, but that's not the whole story, is it, Speed?"

"Not by a long shot, Coach. Gosh, we've got it all over Parkton as far as passing and shooting are concerned. They're a green team. They don't have anybody back from last year. They want to keep the score close and then in the last few minutes of the game—start shootin'! Then, if they get hot—good night!"

"That's right." Coach Rockwell was nodding his head. "If they get hot and happen to hit with a few of their shots and you fellows get excited and miss—you're going to lose a game that everybody expects you to win!"

Striking the table with his fist, he emphasized each word: "*I want you to get that ball! And when you get it,* keep it until you get a good shot under the basket. The first player who takes a heave shot is going to come out of the game—and *stay* out! We've got to play this one smart. Keep in mind that you're two points behind. That means you've got to play heads-up on the defense. You'll get ahead—I know that, but not by taking hope shots. Understand? Lefty? Buzz? Taps? All right then!"

The boys listened intently as Coach Rockwell went on.

"Now, when we get ahead, we'll use the freeze!"

He turned to the blackboard and quickly drew the outline of the front half of a basketball court on the surface. He explained that they must be sure to get the ball across the middle line in ten seconds and be sure to stay in this front half of the court. If they stepped on the center line or a side line, they'd lose the ball.

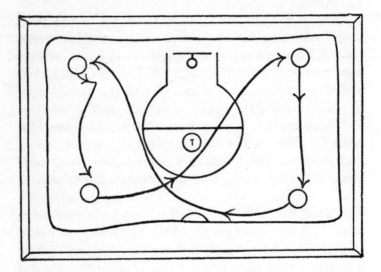

"And be careful of your passes. Keep the ball moving and keep moving yourself. No dribbling, and keep spread out. Remember, they'll be out to steal the ball and they'll double up on you if you don't keep moving.

Taps, you stand in the front half of the free-throw circle." Rockwell turned to the board and placed a T in the circle near the free-throw line. "Be careful—don't let your foot touch the free-throw line or the three-second rule will be in effect and we may lose the ball—

"Follow the paths shown on the board, and I want every player to meet the ball—come to your teammate with the ball. No blind passes! Now, Speed, you've got two time-outs left—use them if you need them. In that last quarter if we get ahead—which we will—we're going to freeze the ball right up to the gun. Understand? We'll give Bill Robbins a little of his own medicine!"

All heads were nodding. They could see now what the coach had meant by playing with your head. There was more to basketball than passing, dribbling, and shooting. No wonder there were so many upsets in basketball. A strange offense or defense, or a planned strategy such as Parkton was using tonight, might easily upset the best team in the state.

Chip glanced down at Taps' ankle. Taps caught his eye and shook his head almost imperceptibly from side to side. His ankle was troubling him. Chip had noticed that in the first half. Parkton's style had made it easier on Taps since he hadn't been forced to do much running. If Coach Robbins found out that Taps had a bad leg, the Parkton center might run him into the ground and out of the game.

The second-half tempo speeded up a bit, but at the end of the third period Parkton was still leading, 16—15. Taps had been going from bad to worse. The Parkton center had discovered that Taps was hurt and was running rings around him.

Shortly after the fourth period started Coach Rockwell removed Taps from the game. There was only a slight spatter of applause for the big center who had looked so bad. Taps had tried to keep from limping, and the fans didn't know he had a bad ankle; they thought he was being outplayed. Bill English reported for Taps. He and the Parkton center were about the same size.

Now the fans were in an uproar; the end of the game was in sight. The Big Reds had to go ahead soon, if they were going to win this game! Speed and Red were trying to set up their pet give-and-go play. They maneuvered slowly and carefully.

Suddenly Speed cut in front of Red, changed direction, and cut hard for the basket. Red looped a high, set-shot pass over the head of Speed's guard who was trailing the speedster in his sudden dash for the goal. It seemed as if the ball were going clear out of bounds, but at the last second Speed leaped high in the air and grasped the ball with his left hand. His body seemed to hang in space as he tried to get control of the ball. With a desperate twist of his body he hooked a one-handed bank shot against the glass backboard, and the ball fell through the hoop to put Valley Falls in the lead for the first time during the game. The crowd went wild.

Speed immediately called time out, and Rockwell substituted the Scott brothers for Buzz Todd and Lefty Peters. Howie and Lennie were expert passers and dribblers but poor shots. The Rock's strategy was obvious to every player on the bench; now it would be Valley Falls' turn to hold the ball if they could get it before Parkton could score.

Parkton brought the ball up the court carefully—too carefully—they were tight and jittery. Speed seemed to be out on his feet. He moved slowly and with apparent effort. He was bent slightly forward, holding his side with one hand; breathing in short, quick gasps, through parted lips.

Chip had seen Speed pull this trick many times; behind this assumed appearance was a hawklike concentration. Then a Parkton player fell for the fake. He threw a cross-court pass toward Speed's opponent, but the ball never reached its mark. Speed shot forward like a streak of lightning, intercepted the ball, and dribbled for the basket. He might have scored, but he didn't try it. His opponent was right on his heels as Speed circled back from the basket and continued the dribble.

Only a minute of play remained, and now Parkton got a dose of its own medicine. Valley Falls was freezing the ball perfectly. Closer and closer the Parkton players pressed, but Lennie, Howie, Red, and Speed were passing beautifully.

Then Bill English brought dismay to every Valley Falls rooter in the gym—he fouled a Parkton player. Bill had been trying to keep out of the way but had collided with an opponent and a foul was called against him for charging.

As the players moved down the floor to the Parkton

basket Coach Rockwell sent Soapy Smith in for English. The move surprised Soapy and everyone else—Soapy was the slowest man on the team.

The crowd was deathly still as the Parkton center moved to the free-throw line. Scarcely pausing he dropped the ball cleanly through the net—the score was tied. The crowd went wild. Thirty seconds left to play—Valley Falls' ball. Speed passed to Red; Red to Howie; Howie to Lennie; then over to Speed who glanced at the clock and dribbled toward the corner. Soapy was moving back and forth directly under the basket trying to gain a good pivot position.

Chip was thinking how many times he had maneuvered for a good pivot position under the basket. Those long hours of practice under the old basket at home had served to make him the highest scorer in the state. Soapy was too slow. . . .

Speed was standing still now—holding the ball and looking up at the big clock. When it showed five seconds to play, he faked a set shot and hooked the ball to Soapy. Soapy leaped high in the air, but before he had a chance to shoot the Parkton center fouled him.

There were less than two seconds left to play when Soapy walked to the foul line; he held the game in the palm of his hand.

Chip looked at Rockwell. If Coach could only substitute someone for Soapy now . . . someone to shoot the foul. But that couldn't be done. The rules didn't permit it. The player fouled had to try for the free throw before a substitute could take his place.

Rockwell was leaning over, hands covering his face, looking steadily down at the floor. Soapy, standing on the free-throw line, turned toward the players on the bench and grinned. Chip could have killed him!

The referee handed the ball to Soapy. Rockwell lifted his head slightly and peeked out between his spread fingers.

Nonchalantly, as if nothing were of any importance, Soapy smiled once more toward the bench and bounced the ball on the floor. Then he winked confidently toward Coach Rockwell and threw the ball right through the basket! The game was over! Valley Falls 18—Parkton 17.

The ending of the game was the signal for the mob to rush Soapy. The players on the floor and those on the bench ganged Soapy before he could move away from the free-throw line. He was thoroughly mauled, hit on the head, punched on the back, shoved, slapped, and roughed up all the way to the dressing room. But he didn't seem to mind; he kept grinning and saying: "You can't hurt me by hittin' me on the head!"

CHAPTER 14

COACH ROCKWELL
SPEAKS HIS MIND

Chip paused outside Coach Rockwell's office. He had decided to tell the coach about Taps' ankle. He was busy with his thoughts and absent-mindedly barged right into Coach Rockwell's office—

"—I happen to know that his family is moving to town, Hank. What's more, I'm giving his old man a job." Jerry Davis, one of Valley Falls' staunchest sports fans, was speaking. Chip paused uncertainly.

Strained silence hung heavily in the room, and it was an embarrassed Hilton who finally blurted out, "Excuse me—er—Coach. I thought you were alone."

"That's all right, Chip. Come in and sit down."

"I can come back," Chip offered.

"No, sit down!" Rock seemed almost eager to have him there—as if he needed him. . . .

Chip noted the set jaws and flushed face. Coach seemed peeved about something.

Jerry Davis cleared his throat. "This fellow is really

a center, Rock: six foot seven or eight, two hundred pounds, and moves like a streak. He's just the thing for us. Why, I don't think you'll ever have a chance to get a natural like him again—and the way Speed, Red, and Buzz are playing he's a sure bet to put you into the tournament."

"Nope, can't be done!"

"Well, why?"

"We've never admitted a boy here in the middle of the year and let him play varsity. It just can't be done!"

"But his people are moving to town. If a family moves to a town and the boy is admitted regularly to school, he can play on any team he can make. The state athletic rules contain nothing which restricts a boy from competing under those circumstances."

Davis paused expectantly, but Coach Rockwell said nothing. "Look at Delford," continued Davis, "and that big Red Henry. He transferred there right in the middle of last year and Jenkins played him."

"That's Delford, not Valley Falls!"

"Look at Rutledge: Burger, their big center, played three years at Cortley over in Ohio before he transferred—and he's playing! Nobody's kicking about that, and he's the most talked-of player in the state. Why, he's averaging twenty points a game!"

"Nope, it's still not the same. Burger started school at Rutledge in September. Why—is none of my business. If this boy—whatever his name is—had come here in September, okay. But nothing doing in the middle of the year."

"But I can't see what difference it makes if he wants to come. He is moving to town soon. The new term starts in February. His coach has already released him; he isn't even playing over at Cortley now."

"I'm not interested! If he wants to come here and go to school, okay! He can play next year. But we're not going to let any boy transfer here in the middle of the season and play basketball—that's final!"

"Well, you're the coach, but you're making a big mistake. If you use Myers, you'll be in the tournament by a mile. Why, he gets better every game he plays! Wait and see!"

Chip wished he could tell them about Taps' ankle. If Coach thought he was "coming along," what would he think if he knew Taps had been playing all along with a bad ankle?

"But we need an experienced center," Davis persisted.

"Not that bad!"

"It happens every year. Why, it isn't fair to keep the boy from playing. There's no ruling which prohibits a kid from playing when his family moves to a town and he enters at the beginning of a term."

"Okay, but it's not going to happen here. Besides, it would be getting around the very principle that led to the formation of the State Athletic Association."

"Well, then, Hank, why didn't they bar Krieger at Bloomfield?"

"I don't know, Jerry." Coach Rockwell stood up and moved toward the door. His attitude plainly expressed his lack of interest in further discussion. "Drop in again sometime!"

"Okay! I guess you know what you're doing. Hello, Hilton; so long, Hank."

Coach Rockwell swung around and looked at Chip. "How's it going?"

"Pretty good after that Parkton game, Coach."

"Yes, that gave us all a lift. You heard what Jerry Davis had to say about Taps Browning, didn't you?"

"Yes, I did, Coach, and—" Chip's thoughts flashed to Taps and his ankle. Davis thought Taps was going to be a flop. Maybe Coach did, too. . . . Well, here goes . . . I might as well get it over with. . . .

"Coach, there's something you ought to know."

"What's that, Chip?"

"You know—you know Taps' bad ankle?"

"Yes."

"Coach, Taps' ankle wasn't taped the night of the Batson game."

"What do you mean?"

"You see, Coach, I asked Taps the day after the Batson game what was wrong with his ankle and he said he didn't get it taped."

"Why not?" Coach Rockwell bit off the words in a hard voice.

"Taps said he waited a long while, but everybody was so busy he didn't want to bother anyone. He didn't want to be the last one out on the floor either—so he let it go."

"A fine thing!" Coach Rockwell's face was flushed.

"That's a fine thing! Chet's supposed to check all the ankles; Pop, too. And by the way, what were you thinking about that night? You're supposed to help out, too!"

"It was my fault, Coach. I should have thought about Taps before anybody else."

"A fine thing! No wonder the kid hasn't been able to play. Where's he now?"

"Probably down at the Sugar Bowl, Coach."

"Well, come along. We'll pick him up and go over to see Doc Jones."

Coach Rockwell's driving and general attitude plainly discouraged conversation.

A little later they stood watching Doc Jones patiently examine Taps' ankle. "Yes, Hank, I know," said Doc Jones, "I took care of the ankle. It's coming along all right."

"Why didn't you tell me about it?" fumed the coach.

"There wasn't anything you could do, Hank. A sprained ankle is a sprained ankle—takes time!"

"I understand that, but what I *don't* understand is why I wasn't told about it. The school physician, Chet, Pop, Hilton, here—everyone knew about the ankle except me. *I'm* just the coach! I suppose I'll have to start taping ankles next!" He glared at Browning. "Why didn't you tell me?" Without waiting for an answer he turned again to Doc Jones.

"Did you take an X ray?" he asked.

"No. I didn't think it was necessary."

"Well, take one!" He paused at the door. "While you're at it, X-ray Hilton's ankle, too. Let's see what that leg of his looks like." He closed the door with a crash and they all breathed a sigh of relief. But it was short-lived. The door was suddenly yanked open just enough to admit Coach Rockwell's head.

"X-ray their heads while you're at it, too. Let me know what's rattling around up there!"

CHAPTER 15

SHARPSHOOTERS

CHIP made his way to the corner of the school cafeteria where the athletes usually gathered and placed his tray on a chair next to Biggie Cohen.

"Hiya, Chip," Biggie said. Then leaning close to Chip he whispered, "I've got some bad news about Fats Ohlsen."

"You punch him?"

"No, course not! His wise stuff is catching up with him, though, at last!"

"What happened?"

"Comin' to school this morning I met Stinky Ferris. He told me about a rooking Fats took in a dice game. Some of those sharpshooters who hang around the Academy took him for a lot of money."

"He can afford it!"

"No, he can't! That's just the point. Stinky told me Fats didn't have the money and gave them some checks. He said Fats is worried sick and is thinking

124

about leaving home, because he didn't have any money in the bank."

"How much did he lose?"

"Nearly a thousand dollars!"

"A *thousand* dollars! Smokes!" Chip's mouth fell open and he gazed at Biggie in amazement. "A thousand dollars," he repeated slowly.

"That's what Stinky said. Stinky wants you and me to see the Rock and get him to straighten it out."

"Wants you and me to see Rock?" Chip gazed at Biggie incredulously. "*You* and *me?* Feeling the way *we* do? That's the best one yet. Huh! Fat chance!"

"I know, Chip. I felt that way, too, but I've been thinking it over all morning. Guess I've got plenty reason to hate that guy, but there's more to it than Fats Ohlsen."

"I can't see it," Chip shook his head from side to side. His lips were set in a thin, straight line. "Why doesn't Stinky go see the coach himself?"

"He's afraid Fats will get sore at him. Look, Chip, Fats Ohlsen means nothing to me. I never did like the guy, but something's got to be done about those gamblers down there. They never work. Simply hang around and take money away from a lot of the pottery guys who can't afford it. Besides, lots of the fellows here in school think they're *something!* Some of the guys even try to dress like 'em. Somebody's got to do something about it, and the Rock's the one that can do it! He hates that whole gang."

"They ought to close the place," Chip muttered.

"What do you say to seeing Rockwell?" Biggie persisted.

Chip shrugged his shoulders. "I'll go along—but I don't feel too good about it."

Coach Rockwell greeted Biggie and Chip with a smile. "Well, what brings you two around here at lunch hour? Good to see you, Biggie. Where've you been keeping yourself?"

"Workin' and studying, Coach. Don't need a good standing guard, do you?"

Coach Rockwell shook his fist at Biggie and smiled. "I thought we decided two years ago that," he paused and winked at Chip before continuing "—as a basketball player you're a pretty good tackle."

"Thanks for the compliment, Coach."

"You don't do bad in baseball though, Biggie. Now, what's on your mind?"

Coach Rockwell soon knew the whole story. He sat in silence for a long time before speaking. "I don't know whether or not this is any of my business. I've warned all you fellows many times to stay away from that place. Other students, too. Of course, Ohlsen hasn't been out for athletics since I bounced him off the football squad last fall. I haven't had much chance to talk to him about his personal life since we had to part company. I doubt whether he would relish my horning in on his private problems, now. Yet I think his father should know about this."

"Don't do that, Coach!" Biggie was distressed. "I promised Stinky I wouldn't tell anyone but Chip and you about it."

"How about those fellows who hang around the pool-room—they all know about it, don't they?"

"I don't think so, Coach. Anyway, they wouldn't want J. P. to know about it any more than Fats would— J. P.'d probably run a crusade and close the place. They sure don't want that!"

Coach Rockwell rubbed his ear vigorously. "Okay, you boys let me see what I can do." After the two boys had gone, Rockwell thumped his desk with a heavy fist. "That's the trouble with some people," he growled aloud, "spoiling their kids with a lot of money. No boy should have money unless he earns it himself. Then he'd learn how to take care of it!"

Late that night, Coach Henry Rockwell paid a visit to the Academy. Mike Sorelli looked up in surprise. He had been one of the veteran coach's boosters for many years. But this was the first time Rockwell had ever been in the Academy. Rockwell glanced quickly back along the chairs lining the walls and then at the clock. It was eleven-thirty.

"Why, hello, Coach. Don't tell me you want to play a game of pool?"

"No, Mike, I don't want to play pool. I came down here tonight to see you about something more important."

"What is it, Coach? You can count on me!"

"I hope I can. You know Joel Ohlsen, I guess—"

"You mean Fats Ohlsen? Sure! Why?"

"Only one reason—and I think you know it. Some of the fellows who hang out here took that boy for nearly a thousand dollars—and he gave them some checks. He doesn't have the money. I want you to get those checks, Mike."

"Now wait a minute, Coach, that's none of my business. I don't allow gambling in my place. If Fats Ohlsen got mixed up with some gamblers, you can't hold me responsible."

"But they hang out here, Mike. And this is where they made up the deal."

"Fats Ohlsen is big enough to take care of himself!"

"True enough, Mike, but not old enough. I expect you to get those checks. If you don't, you're going to be in for a lot of trouble."

"But what have I got to do with it, Coach? Fats Ohlsen comes in here to play pool. So what? No one ever played cards or shot dice in my place and I don't gamble—"

"The fellows who took those checks come in here," interrupted Rockwell, "and a lot of high school kids come in here, too. Those men knew they were playing with a kid—and both you and I know they don't have any business gambling with youngsters."

"Look, Coach, I heard something about it, but it's none of my business. But if you say so, I'll find out about it and let you know the score."

"I don't want to know the score. I want those checks!"

"What am I supposed to do—make up Fats Ohlsen's losses? *I* didn't have nothing to do with it!"

"Now you listen to me, Mike Sorelli. That game started right here in this poolroom. In the first place, you shouldn't let the kids hang out here. You've got the pottery business and that's enough! Those men work for their money and know how to take care of it. Maybe you don't want to keep this poolroom open. If you don't, then just keep on letting those characters who hang out here associate with high school kids."

"Look, Coach, you got it all wrong!"

"Mike, you know the type of fellow who hangs out here better than I do. When they take advantage of a kid who meets them here—that's your responsibility!"

"Look, Coach!" Mike was desperate. "Look! I can't keep high school kids from walking in here. I never let 'em play in no games, Coach."

"They're not supposed to come in here, and playing has nothing to do with it."

"I know, Coach, but they'll think I'm picking on 'em." Mike was squirming. "Anyway, I ain't got no legal right to keep 'em out!"

"That's true, Mike. No legal right! But you do have a moral right. Furthermore, I was always under the impression that you were back of Valley's teams; that you knew that any boy who broke the rules would be dropped from the team; and that you knew that dropping a boy from a team often meant the ruination of a good season. Guess I was wrong about you, Mike!"

"No, you weren't, Coach! Honest! I'd do anything for the team—for you, too, far's that's concerned. Whatever you say goes—I'll make a lot of enemies, I suppose. But from here on—they're gonna stay out!"

CHAPTER 16

THE MISSING BOX

IT WAS the first practice day of the new term. Examinations were over. Some members of the squad had slipped through by the skin of their teeth. But there was a general feeling of rejoicing that the team was intact despite every effort of the faculty. Everybody was feeling fine. There was considerable chatter and laughter and horseplay on the bleachers where Chip had gathered the squad.

Chip should have known by the stern look on Coach Rockwell's face when he came through the door that something grave had happened. Then the stunning blow fell.

"Sanders, turn in your uniform!" The coach's words were spoken quietly and firmly.

Chip heard a gasp of surprise and dismay from the huddle of boys on the bleachers. He looked at little Mike Sanders. The boy's face was as pale as death. A moment later he was at the door. Chip caught a glimpse of his face as he blunderingly reached for the knob. His eyes were blinded with tears. What had happened? Why, Mike had been the find of the season! He had been a sensation against Batson, and now with the Weston game only three days away, he had been dropped from the squad!

Coach Rockwell shuffled his scouting notes and plunged right into a discussion of the game with Weston, as though nothing had happened.

"Now, boys, Weston uses a strict man-to-man defense. Not much switching. This Weston team doesn't have to switch much; they keep on top of you all the time. You're going to have to move against this team or they'll put you in their pockets—

"Hilton, I want you to take English this afternoon and coach him to play just like Fraling. You've played against Fraling several times and you know all his tricks. Make Bill do everything Fraling does—

"Lennie and Howie, you two boys are going to be Benson and Young." Coach Rockwell accentuated his words, tapping the chalk on the blackboard, as he continued. "Don't forget—these two fellows along with Fraling do all the scoring for Weston. The other two men on their team stay in the backcourt and take care of their defense—

"Chet, take these boys out on the court and practice everything you and I discussed this morning. Chip, you concentrate on English. We've got to stop Fraling. As soon as you are sure English knows all of Fraling's stuff, Chet will scrimmage him against Browning. Taps, you go along with Hilton and English and watch everything they do."

Out on the court Chip's thoughts jumped back to Sanders. How had Coach Rockwell known about Mike? Glory . . . the gang might even think I told Coach. . . . Mike is a great guy. . . . His father's dead and there are a half-dozen kids at home. Mike's been playing outside ball, all right. . . . Most all the fellows knew it . . . figured he'd get caught. . . . The ten bucks he gets goes right home . . . well, there just wasn't any middle ground with the Rock. Sanders played outside ball . . . the coach found it out . . . and Mike was through. . . .

For half an hour Chet Stewart worked with the players who represented the Weston team. Chip drilled Bill English over and over on all the tricks for which the big Weston center was famous. Chip knew Fraling inside and out. He had played against him as a sophomore, but the big fellow was a much-improved player now. Taps followed every move and occasionally asked pertinent questions. Chip could hardly wait until he could get to work on Taps at home. Boy . . . ankle or no ankle . . . Taps just had to turn in a good game Friday. . . . Chip Hilton was assuming that responsibility. . . .

Friday night of that week was one long to be remembered. There hadn't been a game like it in Valley Falls for years. It was one for the book; one that would be talked about over and over again. Although the game had ended half an hour before, the crowd was still standing around in the gym and in the halls. The fans just wouldn't go home. Every once in a while someone would let out a whoop and then the whole crowd would start cheering again.

Valley Falls had beaten Weston! Yes, WESTON! The *Cardinals!* Undefeated for two straight years, Weston had lost to the Big Reds tonight chiefly because of the scoring of little Lefty Peters and the defensive play of big Taps Browning. Fraling, the Cardinal's big center, hadn't scored a point! It was unbelievable!

Outside in the hall, friends, parents, and students were waiting for their particular heroes to come out of the dressing room. It was a great night.

Coach had grabbed Chip as soon as he entered the room. "Nice going! Taps told me about those home practice sessions you and he went through to stop Fraling. You sure did it, kid!"

"I didn't do anything, Coach. Taps—"

Coach Rockwell never heard him. He had moved away and was slapping Taps on the back and yelling something to Speed. Speed had Lefty by the hair. "That's what he did," he yelled. "He scalped 'em!"

"One-handed, too," someone hollered.

"Yeah, left-handed," yelled Speed.

Everyone had been worried when Coach Rockwell dropped Mike Sanders, but tonight Lefty Peters had proved himself. Yes, Lefty had scored sixteen points and the winning basket with seconds to go.

Soapy was repeating over and over, "That ball acted

like it had eyes when Lefty threw it. Yes, sir, it *did* have eyes!"

Yes, Valley Falls had beaten the great Weston team, state champions, undefeated for thirty-eight games. They had beaten the Cardinals, 39—38, on little Lefty Peters' last-minute, one-handed throw from the backcourt, and because Taps Browning had played unbelievable defensive basketball and scored five baskets and two fouls to take second place in the scoring with twelve points.

"Aw, that last basket was lucky," Lefty kept saying.

Coach Rockwell had used only six players in the game: Morris, Browning, Schwartz, Todd, and little Lefty Peters had started the game. These five had played the full thirty-two minutes except for Morris, who had been relieved by Soapy Smith for less than a minute midway in the final quarter. Up to then Morris, Schwartz, and Todd had been bottled up completely. Between them they had garnered only eleven points. Taps Browning and Lefty Peters had scored twenty-eight points.

Coach Rockwell and Morris had stood on the side lines briefly and then Speed had dashed back into the game to call a time-out and instruct the gang to freeze the ball the last minute of play if they were ahead. However, Weston had taken a one-point lead seconds later and it was the Cardinals who tried to hold the ball the last minute of play. Five seconds before the end of the game, Lefty Peters had intercepted a Weston pass and, standing way in the backcourt, had thrown the ball like a baseball for the basket. Everyone knew the rest—the ball had smacked against the backboard and dropped through the hoop.

Carrying the tin box which contained the gate receipts, Chip was stopped in the hall by the *Yellow Jacket* reporters who wanted to look at the scorebook. He placed the cash box on the table and soon became completely engrossed in answering their questions and explaining the symbols which described the game.

Some time later Chip picked up the scorebook and started toward the dressing room. Then he remembered the cash box. He hurried back to the table, but the box had disappeared. Maybe he had left it in the box office . . . but, no, he remembered placing the box on the table. . . .

The box office was closed, deserted. He barged upstairs to Rogers' office. Rogers wasn't there. Chip hurried back to the dressing room and searched frantically through his locker, under the rubbing table, in the big waste can, and then rushed into Pop Brown's storeroom. Old Pop gazed at Chip with startled eyes. "What's the matter, Chipper?"

"The money box, Pop! The money box—it's gone!"

"Gone? Where?"

But Chip had hurried back upstairs and out into the gym. There wasn't a thing on the scorer's table. He glanced along the row of bleachers. Only a few enthusiastic fans remained. Looking beyond them, he spied Rogers talking to Coach Rockwell near the door leading to the hall. He looked fearfully from one to the other, but there was no evidence of the box. He approached them with a great fear in his heart. The box *was* gone!

A half-hour of futile searching by Rogers, Coach Rockwell, Chet Stewart, Old Pop, Mr. Anderson, the building superintendent, and Speed, followed—but no box.

Two hours later Chip and Speed started home. The silent ride was broken only by Speed's futile attempts to cheer up his friend. Chip had been thrilled beyond words by the great victory . . . beyond thinking . . . too, he accused himself bitterly. There had been over fourteen hundred dollars in that box. . . . *Fourteen hundred dollars!* . . .

It was a heartsick boy who turned and tossed all that night. He relived every second that had passed since he had placed the box on the table. . . . Who *had* been in that little crowd? . . . Who could have taken the box? Even Coach Rockwell's encouraging "Oh, it'll turn up in the morning" was no comfort.

So passed one of the blackest nights in Chip Hilton's young life.

CHAPTER 17

VF TAKES TO THE ROAD

Coach Rockwell had just finished painting a big white "X" on the gym floor to mark the spot of Lefty Peters' great shot when Chip approached him. Sitting back on his haunches the coach studied Chip, who was shifting his weight from the bad leg to the good one and back again. He startled Chip with a sudden torrent of words. His words were like the clicking of a typewriter: sharp and clear, and tumbling one over the other.

"Now you listen to me, young man! I won't have any more of this foolish talk. Everyone knows you are sorry. We all know you would like to make good the loss; pay it out of your Sugar Bowl wages. So what? Things like this happen many times during a coaching career.

"Don't you think Burrell Rogers and I know how to handle matters of this kind? That's part of our jobs. We carry insurance for just such eventualities, and besides, the Athletic Association has enough money in the bank to take care of the matter without any help from William Hilton!" He daubed paint furiously on the floor.

"We've got to win *two* of those three games on the road trip, if we're going to go anywhere in our division. Maybe if you quit crying on everyone's shoulder about that stupid box you'll have time to look after your manager's job and get things set right for the trip, as you should!"

Chip's face flushed, and his eyes narrowed as the sharp words struck home. Then he caught the friendly glint in the watchful eyes. The red deepened still further. What was the matter with him? Coach was needling him because he was acting like a baby. . . .

"I get it!" he said.

As they walked toward the storeroom he recalled the days which had passed since the Weston game. He hadn't been able to think about anything except the missing box. His mother had laughed it off . . . "Don't worry about it, Chip. We can pay it back—easy!" Coach was right . . . mooning around wouldn't do any good. . . .

His thoughts were interrupted by the coach's voice: "Managing's pretty tough, isn't it, boy?"

"Times like this it is." Chip smiled wryly. "Guess it isn't as hard as coaching, though," he ventured.

"What makes you think coaching is so bad?"

"Well, it doesn't seem to be very much fun. When you win, they say you should have won by a larger score, and when you lose—you're Public Enemy Number One."

"Yes, but there're some compensations that more than make up for that—"

"You mean the team?"

"Sure! Watching kids like you come along, develop initiative and courage and sportsmanship. Why, it's the best job in the world!"

Thursday morning, Chip made his way through the milling crowd in the railroad station and joined Coach Rockwell, Chet Stewart, and the team at the information booth.

"All set, Chip?"

"Everything's checked, Coach. I've got the tickets right here."

"Keep them! It's your responsibility to get us where we're going, you know!"

"And back, too," added Stewart. "Let's go!"

Chip led the way along the platform until he came to car 519. The Big Reds took over then, stowing bags, shedding coats, laughing, shouting, talking. Chip swung his chair around so that he was facing Taps. He felt good today. The train slid quietly forward—they were on their way—on a trip that could make or break the chances for the Big Red team.

Three days later a jubilant Big Red team was homeward bound once more. The trip, which had started off badly with the unexpected loss to Parkton by a 21—20 score, had wound up in a blaze of glory. Coach Rockwell's words were clicking almost as fast as the rails beneath the lounge car. Yes, Coach was happy today! So was Chip—so was everybody! They had won the last two games of the trip!

On Friday night they had taken Hampton, 39—38, and the very next night had beaten the Sailors, 41—32.

Chet Stewart, Chip, Red, Speed, and Taps were listening intently to Rockwell's words: "We learned something on this trip, Chet. Bill English proved a big man could be stopped from the front. Taps, you want to keep that in mind. Some of the big centers coming up may be a little too tough to play from the back."

"How about Delford's Red Henry?" asked Chet.

"Right!" agreed the coach. "He's too big to play straight."

"Speed and Red sure had their eyes on the old hoop —didn't they, Coach?" Chip was beaming.

"Don't forget those set shots of Soapy's!" Speed interrupted. "Old Soapy's really got the set shot licked."

"He's coming along," agreed Coach Rockwell. "Wonder how he developed it so fast?"

Speed laughed. "He didn't develop it!" he said. "Chip's responsible. He's had Soapy over behind the house every day, rain or shine, and then he takes Soapy up to the Y every night for an hour."

"Yeah, and every Saturday, too," added Red Schwartz.

"A good thing we had Soapy along," Chet Stewart nodded gratefully.

"He was great!" added Chip. "Say, Coach, wouldn't a zone defense have stopped Parkton?"

"We'd have used a zone if necessary, Chip, but I'd rather hold up our special defenses until we really need them. Don't forget it wasn't our defense that whipped us at Parkton—it was our offense."

"Boy, I sure feel better today than I did on Thursday!" Chet Stewart breathed a joyful sigh.

"I guess we all do," Coach Rockwell agreed. "Can you imagine how we would have felt coming back to Valley Falls if we'd lost all three games?"

"They'd probably have run us out of town!" Chet laughed.

"Probably will, anyway." Coach Rockwell smiled. "They're hard to please!"

Valley Falls was "hoop" crazy! The Big Reds were on fire. Following the Salem game, Valley Falls had walked all over Steeltown, Hampton, Dulane, and Northville. The victories over Hampton, Dulane, and Northville were expected, but no one except Soapy Smith had figured the Big Reds to take Steeltown. To-day, Washington's Birthday, they were leaving on the second road trip of the season and the one which would have an important bearing on their chances for Sectional honors.

It seemed as if the whole town in holiday mood was at the bus station. The students and townfolks were holding an impromptu rally, and crowds surrounded the big bus while pictures were being taken. They were yelling, cheering, and giving the team a real send-off this time. Past mistakes and disappointments were forgotten. The town and the school were proud of its team. Everybody loves a winner!

The bus was a beauty all right: decorated in red and white, pennants flying, and with the big "Special" spelled out in the front. Special it was, too!

This trip might well be one to remember; the team record was now eight, nine if you counted the Alumni game, victories and two defeats. Everyone was talking about the Big Reds and the state championship. Could be, too, Chip thought, if we win on the road!

"Bring back the bacon!" "Keep punching, gang!" "Look out for those Cardinals!" "We'll be watching you!" "Don't let Soapy jump out!"

Then everyone was hollering and waving and the bus was moving; the gang let out a great cheer and they were on their way again. Soapy was bouncing up and down in his seat yelling, "Here we go again, gang. An' this time we're really rollin'!"

The arrival at Cary seemed almost a repeat story of their departure from Valley Falls. Tech's big band at the hotel was brassy and loud and the crowd cheered them again and again.

"You'd think we were state champs," said Speed.

"Could be, pal! Could be," said Red.

"Could be, nothing," broke in Soapy. "We is, pal. We *is!*"

They all piled out of the bus and gathered in front of the desk in the hotel lobby. Chip had the room keys, but before passing them out, he got everyone's attention and read Coach Rockwell's schedule:

" 'Lunch at one c'clock. Skull practice at two-thirty. Everyone in bed from three until four-thirty. Pre-game snack—five o'clock. Five-thirty: ten-minute hike. Five forty-five: back to bed. Seven o'clock we meet in the lobby and go out and beat Tech!' "

Everyone cheered. Spirit was high!

Pausing in his letter writing, Chip looked across the

room toward the bed from which the faint snore had come. "What a guy!" he breathed. "In bed and sound asleep at this hour—" He looked at his watch. It was just ten o'clock. He continued with the letter to his mother. A little later he sealed and stamped the letter and glanced again at Taps—dead to the world. Chip was a little tired, too. He leaned back in the chair.

What a trip this had been! Soapy was right. . . . The Big Reds *were* rolling; and rolling up the scores, too! They'd been right at home on Tech's big court and had walked away with the game, 45—30. Stratford had been tough—for three quarters. Then Speed and Red had gone to work with their give-and-go plays and there was nothing to it. . . . Speed scored sixteen points and Red got fourteen. . . . Their total was more than that of the whole Stratford team. Valley Falls 36—Stratford 28. . . .

Chip heaved a sigh of satisfaction. Two down and only Weston to go! Yes . . . only the Cardinals. But the Cardinals would be *really* tough at home. . . . You could bet they hadn't forgotten that first defeat in two years. They'd be out to even up with the Big Reds tomorrow night. . . .

Everything was swell . . . no . . . not everything. He hadn't completely forgotten the money box . . . that three-weeks-old mystery still remained unsolved. Coach Rockwell had kept him so busy lately, he'd hardly had time to think. . . . Who *had* been in that crowd by the table? Harry Nichols and Ted Williams . . . Joe Kennedy of the *Times* . . . Pete Williams of the *Post* . . . Stinky Ferris . . . *and* Fats Ohlsen!

He jumped as the telephone shrilled. It was Chet Stewart.

"Chip?"

"Yes, Chet."

"Check all the rooms—see that everyone's in and report back."

"Sure, Chet, right away."

Chip hurried along the halls, knocking on the doors of the rooms he had listed. "Open up, you guys. Get to bed! Get some sleep!"

"Okay, Chip!"

"Got to win that game tomorrow."

"It's a cinch—just a pushover, Chip, old kid," called Speed as Chip hurried down the hall.

The players always paired up on the trip. Chip and Taps usually roomed together. At Room 1214 he got no answer. He checked the list; yes, it was the room which had been assigned to Buzz Todd and Lefty Peters. He knocked several times, but still there was no answer. What was the matter? He went back to his room and called Room 1214 on the telephone. Still no answer.

Gosh . . . Stewart had said to report right back. . . . He was probably waiting right now for the call. What to do? What *could* he do? What could he tell Chet?

It was ten minutes after eleven by his watch. He'd try the lobby. . . . No luck! He'd call once more. . . . Better check the hotel register. . . . Nope, his room list was correct. Now he *had* to report to Stewart . . .

"Come in, Chip. All check?"

"Went to every room, Chet."

"That's good. Thanks, Chipper, you'd better get some sleep yourself. See you in the morning."

Outside the door Chip paused. "There I go again," he muttered. "If Coach Rockwell finds out about this he'll never trust me any more. What makes me think he trusts me now? He knows I'm responsible . . . so does the whole school. I've just got to get that box. Fats was right beside it. He *could* be the one . . . he needed the money to get the checks. He *must* have taken it! I'm going to see J. P. Ohlsen . . . and I don't mean Joel Palmer Ohlsen, Jr. . . ."

Back in his room he called Buzz and Lefty's room again. Still no answer! What had happened to those two? What a spot to be in. . . .

Next morning Chip hurried down to Room 1214 and banged on the door. Buzz Todd greeted him cheerily. Chip wasted no time.

"Where'd you guys go last night?" he asked, looking from one to the other.

"Show. Why?" asked Buzz nonchalantly.

"Why?" demanded Chip angrily. "Why? Because everyone was supposed to be in bed by eleven o'clock —that's *why!*"

"We lost track of the time, Chip. The show was late," Lefty apologized lamely.

"You knew the show would be late and you knew you were supposed to be in, too! What's the matter with you, anyway?" Chip glared at him and then snapped, "You know how Rock is about things like that!"

"Does he know we weren't in?" Buzz asked, alarmed.

"No, he doesn't! Chet asked me to check and report, but I didn't tell him."

"Gosh, Chip, thanks."

"Don't thank me! I don't want any thanks for that! I had to let Chet Stewart down just because you weren't sports enough to get in on time. 'Specially the night before the most important game on the schedule."

"Sorry, Chip, it won't happen again."

Chip slammed the door and joined the crowd down in the lobby.

Coach Rockwell and Chet Stewart were seated over in one corner, talking quietly.

"What time did you say they got in, Coach?" Stewart was puzzled.

"I saw them about a quarter to twelve. Just the two of them."

"Do you think they had just gone out?"

"No," said Coach Rockwell, "I think they were just coming in. Probably been to a show."

"See *you?*"

"Don't think so. They were pretty much in a hurry."

"Wonder why Chip didn't tell me?"

"Did you expect him to, Chet?" Rockwell regarded Stewart quizzically. "You made a mistake there, Chet. Never ask a kid to check up on his teammates; it isn't fair!" His voice was just a bit sharp as he concluded, "Forget the whole thing! I don't go for tattletales!"

What a team! Everybody in Valley Falls was slapping the kids on the back and talking about the tournament.

Hadn't the Big Reds beaten Weston again! And on their own floor? The first team to beat the Cardinals on their own floor in seven years! Yep, it took the Rock and Valley Falls to do the unexpected. Hadn't they won all three of the road games on this trip; two out of three on the first one? That was playing ball! Wait until the tournament! Section Two was just as good as wrapped up. What if they were tied with Weston and eleven victories and two defeats. Hadn't they given Weston those two defeats? Sure, they had! What was more, the last game at Weston had been decisive. They'd beaten the Cardinals 53—41. The Big Reds were a cinch to win the state tournament this year!

Yes, Valley Falls was back in the fight for state honors. There was just a little bit of swagger when the fans talked about the Big Reds now. The players swaggered a bit, too.

But there were two interested persons who weren't swaggering, Coach Rockwell and Chet Stewart. The two mentors were seated in the athletic office. Stewart was looking out the window, his eyes focused on the big stadium back of the gym. Coach Rockwell was sitting behind his desk, fingering a sheaf of newspaper clippings.

Stewart broke the silence. "They're pretty cocky, Coach! They're pretty cocky!"

"I know, Chet. I know they are. Most kids would feel pretty good if they read all this junk." He shoved the sports write-ups aside.

"What are you gonna do about it?" Chet worried.

"Nothing right now, I guess. Sometimes a team needs a lot of confidence. Sometimes it helps!"

"Yeah, but this is the wrong kind of confidence, Coach. They think they're world-beaters!" Chet was disgusted. "Who do they think they are? Why don't you slap them down a bit? That's what you used to do to us," he said hopefully.

"Maybe so, Chet, but there isn't much rhyme or reason trying to compare boys of today with kids of your time and mine. Everything changes."

Everything but you, Coach." Chet laughed. "You'll never change!"

CHAPTER 18

THE HARDER
THEY FALL

SOUTHERN's team was made up of five kids who had played together all through grade school. They had entered high school as a group and had made history as Southern's reserve team. Now the varsity, they played like champions. Their team play was perfect and time and time again they dashed down the floor to score easy points with their quick-break attack. Todd and Peters were caught out of position again and again.

Chip, at the scorer's table, was squirming, pushing, elbowing, and making every play. Why didn't Coach do something . . . what was wrong with Speed . . . why didn't he call for a time-out? . . .

Just then, as if by mental telepathy, Speed called, "Time!"

Chip looked at the scoreboard and the clock. Southern 40—Valley Falls 22. Eighteen points behind and twelve minutes to play—couldn't be done. . . .

Coach Rockwell substituted Soapy Smith for Lefty

149

Peters. Soapy, all excited and sputtering, rushed up to Speed. "Coach said to go into a zone right away!"

"A zone?" Speed was bewildered. "A zone with twelve minutes to go and eighteen points behind? Are you sure, Soapy?"

"That's what he said!"

"Okay. Zone it is! But *one* of us is crazy! Now look, you guys—"

For the next six minutes Chip was kept so busy marking down baskets, fouls, and free throws that he never knew the score.

"Hello, folks—this is Stan Gomez—WTKO takes you now to the Valley Falls-Southern High basketball game at Valley Falls. And, believe you me, we're catching the climax of a hectic game. After being behind 40 to 22 with twelve minutes to go, Valley Falls has climbed back into this game—the score now—Southern 44—Valley Falls 41! Two minutes to play—

"Valley Falls' Morris and Schwartz are playing the game of their lives—and Taps Browning, the kid who has been handicapped with a bad ankle all year, seems to have found himself. Speed Morris and Red Schwartz are fighting like madmen under both baskets—Browning is scoring with one-hand jump shots that are reminiscent of Chip Hilton—

"There he goes—up again—and it's *in!* The score now is 44 to 43, Southern leading. Minute and a half to play—Southern has the ball out of bounds now—in to Glasco—he's dribbling down the middle of the court—

he passes to Southern's big center, Ford—there's a foul!
No—not on Valley Falls—on Ford. After Ford received
the ball he turned and shoved Browning with his
elbow—

"Browning is on the free-throw line now—has a
chance to tie this game right now—score is 44 to 43.
Browning shoots—it's *good!* Tie score now, 44 to 44.
Fifty seconds to play—

"It's Southern's ball out of bounds again. They're
bringing the ball up the court—they're trying to hold
it—Valley Falls is waiting—Southern is passing—over
to Glasco—back to Ford—over to Kimmel—the ball is
in the front court now—Valley Falls is gradually pressing Southern back toward the ten-second line. Hold it!
There's a foul! Looks as if it's against Valley Falls—it
is! Coach Whitcomb is on his feet over there—he's
waving to Glasco to shoot the foul. Yep! Glasco is on
the line now—he shoots and—he *misses!* Listen to that
crowd—

"Taps Browning took that rebound—he passes over
to Schwartz—Schwartz is dribbling down the floor—
Morris has the ball now, in the corner—back to
Schwartz it goes—over to Peters—to Todd—Todd dribbles in and—there's a *foul*—on Ford again. Ford
switched to stop Todd and fouled him just before the
shot—Valley Falls has a chance to win this game now—

"Todd is on the line—he's one of the best shots in
the state—the referee hands the ball to Todd—Todd
looks at the clock—only seconds to play now—he
bounces the ball on the floor—he *shoots!* It's *GOOD!*

"Southern's ball now, out of bounds—five seconds to play. There's a long pass—it's *intercepted*—Morris leaped high in the air to grab that ball. There's the gun—the game's over! Valley Falls wins, 45 to 44. What a game!"

Valley Falls' fans couldn't believe it, and Chip, sitting at the scorer's table, wouldn't believe it. Lose to Dane? It was impossible! Why the Danes hadn't won more than four games all year. Everyone had beaten them— that is up until February when Myers, the big transfer center from Cortley, had joined the team.

Dane had taken the lead at the very start of the game and had never been less than ten points ahead. Now in the last quarter Valley Falls was fourteen points behind —and getting nowhere fast.

The Big Reds just couldn't get going. The Scott twins were fighting their heads off, but they made too many mistakes—bad passes, got caught with the ball, didn't pick up quick enough on the defense—didn't switch—

Chip was conscious of someone talking. They were expressing his own thoughts. Smokes! It was his own voice . . . he was talking out loud . . . things *must* be bad! "Why, gosh, even without Buzz and Lefty we ought to beat Dane! They don't have a thing except Myers, and Taps is playing him better than even—"

Chip quickly checked the scorebook. Anxiously scanning the totals he was relieved to see that the book was all in Taps' favor. Taps had scored 13 points and Myers had 7, so far. Points weren't everything, but Taps was passing off well, too, on the pivot, and he was getting his share of the rebounds. . . . Creepers . . . if Myers outplayed Taps . . . Jerry Davis and all the fans would be on Coach Rockwell's neck for not letting Myers transfer to Valley Falls. . . . If only Buzz and Lefty were in there. . . .

Speed and Red were battling furiously. Time and again Speed drove in—trying to pull the game out singlehanded. The Dane guards couldn't hold him, yet there was so little time left to play—

With five minutes to go Soapy Smith was substituted for Lennie Scott. Soapy played like a tiger. He was in every play—fighting, talking, pepping up his team-mates, patting them on the back—urging them to keep going—

The Dane player guarding Soapy floated away to help double-team Morris. Speed rifled the ball to Soapy, who electrified everyone by dropping in a long set shot from the side; minutes later he did it again, and then again—aiming the ball each time as if his life depended upon it. His last goal cut the Dane lead to six points.

Chip was cheering every play, pounding the table and elbowing the Dane scorer on each movement of the ball. Speed scored again, and then Soapy dropped in another set. Chip looked at the time.

The hands of the big clock were speeding relentlessly toward the end of the game. Now only one minute was left to play—two points behind . . . forty seconds . . . thirty seconds . . . twenty! The whistle! A foul!

Chip groaned and buried his head in his hands.

Smokes . . . it's on Speed . . . that's the end! He glanced up just as the ball dropped cleanly through the hoop. Three points behind. Before Valley Falls even had a chance to try another shot the timer's gun ended the game. The final score: Dane 49—Valley Falls 46.

It was a quiet crowd of fans who filed out of the gym and down the steps to the street. Usually the whole neighborhood rang with laughter, shouts, and cheers. Tonight everyone seemed in a hurry. The fans were down. *Way* down!

Why, that very evening, Stan Gomez had "shot the stars" for Valley Falls. They had all listened. Gomez had rated the Big Reds the best team in Section Two— probably the best in the state. Now, not three hours later, that had all gone up in thin air. Valley Falls had lost to the weakest team on its schedule. And on the home court!

"Delford and Salem are next. If we couldn't beat Dane, how can we beat those two? There goes the tournament! . . ."

"Lefty Peters beat Weston almost by himself and Rockwell didn't use him at all tonight. Why, come to think of it, Peters wasn't even dressed! . . ."

"That Dane team doesn't have a thing. If Buzz Todd had been in there we would have beaten them by fifteen points! . . ."

"I hear there's dissension on the team. Too many stars! Too much publicity! . . ."

"What are you talking about? Why, Browning musta got twice as many points as Myers. Played him to a standstill. Myers didn't beat us—it was those Scott kids; they've had no experience. . . ."

"Been readin' their clippin's! Got swelled heads! . . ."

"Rock dropped Todd and Peters just tonight. Broke training, they say. . . ."

"Rockwell's too tough! First he dropped Sanders, and now he's canned Todd and Peters. Just when we looked like a sure thing for the state. . . ."

Chip, Speed, and Taps sat silently in the jalopy. The row of parked cars had departed long since; yet Speed made no move to start his chariot. There was no need to rush down to the Sugar Bowl tonight—

Chip's thoughts turned to Coach Rockwell. Bet he wasn't drawing pictures or writing names this evening. Some of Coach Rockwell's pet philosophies and sayings ran through his mind. . . .

"On the sports pages you're a hero today and the forgotten man tomorrow!" "Success is not measured by the number of lines of publicity you get but by the way you play the game. . . ."

"Some of you fellows have been chasing headlines. The quicker you stop reading the sports columns and start to play basketball—the quicker we'll get back in the winning columns. . . ."

"There are turning points in every game. Some people call those the breaks of the game. They're not breaks. Those turning points are the result of constant concentration by certain players. Some players have the ability to concentrate at all times—winning or losing—

others concentrate only when it means the plaudits of the crowd. The *real* athlete concentrates all the way—permits nothing except the game to enter his mind. That's why *he's* a champion."

Chip's thoughts swung into other channels. Ever since the first road trip he had been trying to decide what course he should pursue with respect to the cash box and Fats Ohlsen. During the month that had elapsed since the theft of the Weston game gate receipts, speculation and talk at Valley Falls High had died down somewhat. It no longer was mentioned in the *Yellow Jacket*. But Chip could not forget it.

No matter how hard he tried to keep his mind off the box it came popping back—and Joel Ohlsen with it!

Telling J. P. about Joel's gambling debt and his suspicions regarding the box seemed like a dirty trick—but something *had* to be done. That box was his responsibility and he wasn't going to fool around any longer. . . .

Right after his football injury, J. P. Ohlsen had said he could always come to him at any time for advice or help . . . well . . . it was time. . . . This was going to hurt. . . .

He considered the possibility of tackling Fats direct. No . . . he wouldn't get to first base that way . . . Fats would laugh at him. Well . . . J. P. wouldn't laugh . . . he'd get action there . . . of one kind or another. . . .

Speed broke the silence. "What are we going to do about Todd and Peters?"

"We've got to do something," Chip replied absentmindedly.

"I don't think Coach will let 'em play any more this year," said Taps. His long legs dangled over the side of the car and his arms, hanging loosely, nearly reached the floor. He was entirely oblivious to the cold; in fact, he hadn't even closed the side door which Speed had managed to tie onto the battered body.

"Someone ought to ask the coach to give 'em another chance," said Speed.

"Stop beating around the bush," said Chip. "You know it's only a question of which one of us is going to talk to the coach. Who's it going to be, the captain or the manager?" Chip proceeded slowly, "I think it should be the captain!"

"Huh! Think I'm crazy?"

"Seems to me it's your responsibility."

"Aw, heck, Chip. You know I can't talk to Rock like you can!"

Chip sat quietly for a long minute. Then he elbowed Speed. "Okay, I'll see him. I'll see somebody else, too. I might as well have a showdown *all* around!"

CHAPTER 19

THE BOX TURNS UP

JOEL OHLSEN's collar was wilted and so was his spirit when he walked out of Coach Rockwell's office. He had just passed through the worst hour of his life. His ears were burning, and his face was fiery red. Although he should have felt happier than he had ever dreamed possible, his heart was heavy. Tightly clasped in his hand he held three pieces of paper; three pink checks totaling nearly a thousand dollars!

Ohlsen was filled with mixed emotions. Relief from the pressure of fear which had been his lot since the night of the dice game; a feeling of shame because of the dressing down Coach Rockwell had just given him, and a glow of thankfulness because his conscience had found rest. Yes, Coach Rockwell had poured it on, but he felt grateful even for that.

Stinky was waiting. "What happened?" he asked breathlessly.

"What happened?" echoed Joel. "Look!" He held out

158

the checks. "That's what happened. What a guy! What a guy!"

"The coach?"

"Sure! Nobody else! I've had him wrong all along." He regarded Stinky thoughtfully. "Guess I've had a lot of things wrong." Joel stopped abruptly. His eyes were puzzled. "Say," he began, "say, you know something?"

"What?"

"Rockwell told me Chip Hilton and Biggie Cohen got him to go down to Mike's and get those checks. I can't understand it! Of all people!"

"Hilton and Cohen?"

"Yeah, Hilton and Cohen. I don't get it!"

"I told you all along they were right guys, Joel."

"I know, Stinky, but right or wrong—those guys ought to hate me. Wonder what made them do a thing like that?" Ohlsen was completely bewildered. "How did *they* find out about it?" he mused aloud.

Stinky didn't answer. He was thinking about Biggie Cohen. Biggie hadn't let him down; Joel didn't know . . .

A sober Ohlsen broke the silence. "Coach said the gamblers had given the checks back of their own accord and that the debt was canceled. Said the whole thing was probably part of a plot to teach me a lesson— wonder if he was kiddin' me?" He paused. "What a sucker I've been!"

Stinky nodded his head. "You were that, all right," he said. "I'm glad now my old man kept *me* out of there."

"Coach made me promise to stay away from there, too, Stinky. And you know what?"

"What?"

"I'm gonna do it! You know what else I'm goin' to do?"

"What?"

"I'm gonna look up Biggie Cohen and Hilton and apologize."

"They'll probably drop dead!"

"Probably'll kill me, too. I never apologized to anyone before in my life. I sure owe those two guys a lot. Makes me feel pretty cheap. Especially after the trick I pulled on Chip Hilton."

"What trick?"

Ohlsen took a deep breath. "You remember the night we beat Weston?"

"Yeah."

"Hear anything about someone stealin' the gate receipts from Hilton that night?"

"Sure! Why?"

"Well—I'm the guy."

"You mean—you mean you took the box? How? When? What'd ya do with it?"

"Remember when we stopped in the hall after the game, and Hilton was showing everyone the scorebook? Well, I saw the box on the table and, well, for some reason I just dropped my topcoat over it and—well, you know the rest."

"What'd you do with it?"

"Still got it! Box and all! Been tryin' to figure out a way to get it back—that is, till this afternoon. First I figured I'd use the money to get back the checks, but something held me back—glad I didn't, now."

Stinky's mouth fell open. "Sufferin' cats!" he managed. "What you gonna do with it?"

Ohlsen didn't answer. He was deep in thought.

"Give it to me, Joel," Stinky whispered. "I'll get it back! I'll slip it up on Rockwell's porch and ring the bell and run."

"Too late, Stinky. I told the coach all about it—I'm to take the box over to his house tonight."

"As I live and breathe!" Stinky gasped.

They stood in silence; each boy busy with his own thoughts.

Joel suddenly squared his shoulders and muttered, "I've got to do it myself! Just got to!"

"Do what?" Stinky asked as Ohlsen started up the hill.

"Tell Joel Palmer Ohlsen, Sr., a mystery story," Fats answered.

All the way home Stinky puzzled over Joel's cryptic remark. As he passed the Academy Pool and Billiard Parlor he checked his thoughts long enough to throw a loud "bronx cheer" in the direction of Mike Sorelli's emporium.

Although it was bitter cold, Chip Hilton was perspiring freely as he sat in the telephone booth.

"But it is a personal matter, Mr. Ohlsen. It's about Joel, and I'd rather see you at your house. It's awfully important. You told me last fall in the hospital to call on you any time—I have to work tonight, sir. I'd rather get it over with this afternoon, right away— It *is* important! It's about Joel, sir— Yes, sir. All right, sir. I'll be there in fifteen minutes!"

Chip trudged up the winding driveway which led to the big Ohlsen mansion. Not many years back he had spent many happy hours on these grounds and at this house. But that was before his father's death and before Fats and he had broken up their grade school friendship.

In those days he had always dashed straight up the big wide steps three at a time, hollering for Joel to "Hurry up!"

Today he had taken the long way—postponing a little longer his coming interview with J. P. Ohlsen. The closer his dragging footsteps brought him to the big house, the lower his heart sank.

J. P.'s big limousine was parked in the side drive as Chip went up the porch steps one at a time. In the library, waiting with a tight chest and a thumping heart, he tried to collect his thoughts and plan his words, but his mind just wouldn't function. For a brief moment he was tempted to cut and run; to make some excuse and leave well enough alone.

"Hello, Chip. I hope there's nothing wrong at home. Sit down."

J. P. smiled warmly and motioned Chip to a chair.

Too late now. Well . . . here goes. . . .

"Thank you, sir. No, sir. Everything's all right at home." Chip gulped, and then plunged.

"Mr. Ohlsen, when I was in the hospital, you said I could always come to you for help at any time—"

"That's right, Chip. What's this all about?"

"Fats, I mean Joel, sir. It's about Joel and the money box."

"Money box? What money box?"

"The money box that was stolen—I mean that disappeared the night of the Weston game—"

"How does that concern Joel, Chip?"

"Well, I—I think Joel took it!" Chip held his breath.

"What's *that?* What did you say? What do you mean?"

"I think Joel took the box, Mr. Ohlsen."

J. P. Ohlsen straightened up in his chair and regarded Hilton with amazement. "What on earth are you talking about? What would Joel want with the box?"

"He needed money, sir. He needed money badly."

"Joel needed money? What for?"

Chip was silent. Finally, under J. P. Ohlsen's stern gaze, he said, "I'd rather not say, sir." Then he added doggedly, "But I *know* he took the box!"

"Why I never heard anything so preposterous in all my life. You're making a very serious accusation, Hilton."

"I know, but—"

In the hall outside the library Joel Ohlsen was listening intently to the conversation in the book-lined room. Under one arm he was clutching the black money box. He breathed deeply, and stepped into the room.

"What he says is true!"

J. P. turned and stared incredulously at his son. His eyes shifted to the box and back again to Joel's face. He shook his head slowly from side to side in bewilderment.

"I don't understand," he said, sinking back in his chair and regarding Joel blankly.

"Everything Chip has said is true!" Joel stated flatly. "I *did* need money, and I *did* take the box! I told Coach Rockwell all about it just a little while ago." He faced his father with a set face and steady eyes.

Chip had risen to his feet and was nervously biting his lips. "I'm—I'm sorry, Joel," he managed. "Honest—"

Joel's determined face relaxed as he turned to Chip. "I'm the one who's sorry, Chip—" His voice broke and he sank into a chair, covering his face with his hands.

J. P. Ohlsen rose from his chair, pressed a trembling hand to his forehead, and moved slowly toward the window. Chip stopped beside Joel just long enough to grip the shaking shoulder. "It's okay, Joel. Everything'll come out all right."

Chip again chose the winding driveway instead of the long flight of steps. In the library window, J. P. Ohlsen watched with empty eyes the dragging steps of the boy who had just brought the worst news ever to cross the big mansion's threshold.

Long after Hilton had passed from view, J. P. stood in the window, living again the past few minutes and the years they represented. His thoughts ranged from this house to the big pottery and back again. The ultimate goal of all the years he had devoted to building up the Valley Falls Pottery to its present position had been to leave his son a proud heritage.

But he had forgotten the most important thing; he had forgotten those important years when his son needed him most. Needed something more than a car, a weekly allowance, and a doting mother.

A growing boy needed the guidance and understanding of a man. . . . But he'd been too busy. . . . Well, he'd *have* to take a hand now. . . . In the past . . . when he had tried to interfere with Mrs. Ohlsen's pampering of Joel . . . his efforts had led to a family quarrel. A quarrel which ended with Joel's mother in tears and Joel in sullen silence. . . .

Joel had shown real courage this afternoon. Maybe it wasn't too late. A change of atmosphere and a curtailment of such luxuries as a car and too much leisure time —maybe a little closer supervision—tighter reins; then the boy's reactions would determine whether he was made of the right stuff! . . .

"Not all the clay that has to be molded is at my pottery," J. P. thought, as he turned to comfort his son.

CHAPTER 20

THE SCORE THAT
COUNTS

As STAN GOMEZ finished his seven o'clock sportscast, Speed Morris reached up and snapped off the radio. "Wonder what's keepin' him?" he asked, glancing around the room at the sober faces. There was no reply. Each boy was busy with his own thoughts.

Practice that afternoon had been terrible. Everyone had expected a real going-over from the coach, but he had said nothing about the Dane game. Chet Stewart had run the squad through medicine-ball calisthenics, several passing and dribbling drills, and then Coach Rockwell had unveiled a new attack formation. But something was missing. The pep and dash; the exuberant and spontaneous yelling; the good-natured kidding—was gone! It was a beaten squad!

After a short, slow-motion workout, Coach Rockwell had dismissed them with a weary "That's all, boys."

In the dressing room Speed had moved from player to player speaking with lowered voice. Later, he had looked up Buzz Todd and Lefty Peters, and now all were gathered in the big living room of the Hilton home.

Chip wasn't there. According to plan he was to see Coach Rockwell right after practice with a plea from the squad for the reinstatement of Buzz and Lefty.

It was nearly nine o'clock before they heard Hilton's dragging steps. Even before he entered the room the worried group of boys knew the answer. All eyes were on Chip as he dropped wearily down on the couch.

"No soap, gang," he said.

"You mean we're through for the season?" Lefty's voice was shaky.

"Looks that way."

"Musta been a tough session," ventured Taps.

"No, just the opposite, Taps. Coach was swell. Said he appreciated how we all felt, but there was nothing he could or would do about it. Said Buzz and Lefty knew the rules same as Mike Sanders did, and they'd have to take the penalty."

"Seems to me it's more like penalizing the team!" said Lennie Scott.

"Seems the same to me!" echoed Howie.

There was a long silence. Buzz Todd was pressing his lips tight together as he gazed dejectedly at Chip, and Lefty Peters was hunched over looking steadily at the floor. Every boy in the room was thinking the same thing—"There goes the tournament!"

Red Schwartz was bitter. "What in the world was he snoopin' around Mike Sorelli's for, anyway?"

Chip could have told Schwartz a lot about *that*. The

Rock must have gone down there again to pick up Fats' checks. Seemed like Fats Ohlsen spelled trouble in more ways than one. If he hadn't gambled, there would have been no bad checks . . . no missing box . . . no session with J. P. like the one this afternoon . . . no need for Coach Rockwell to go to the Academy . . . and Lefty and Buzz would still be on the team. . . .

"It was *my* fault!" Lefty's voice was filled with self-disgust. "We were on our way home, and I thought there wouldn't be any harm in watching the Kelly game a little while. Buzz didn't want to go. We never dreamed we'd run into him."

"How come Mike didn't chase you?" asked Schwartz. "He's been running all the guys out lately."

"He didn't see us—we went in the side door."

"I never dreamed it was so late," said Buzz.

"What time was it?" someone asked.

"Must have been pretty near midnight."

"No wonder the Rock was peeved!" Soapy moaned. "Well, there's no use sittin' here mopin'. We can't quit. We gotta do something!"

"Soapy's got the right idea," said Chip. "We've got to win those next two games."

"Won't do us any good if we do win!" Red growled. "We're already out of the running—with three losses. Steeltown's only got one more game—Southern. They'll murder *them!*"

"Don't be too sure about that," said Chip. "Don't forget Southern gave us a real going-over and we had Buzz and Lefty playin', too. They might do it!"

"Southern'll beat Steeltown!" Soapy looked challengingly at Schwartz. "I can feel it!"

"Won't make any difference unless we beat Delford and Salem," said Chip. "Let's concentrate on them; what say, gang?"

"The Scotts can do it!" said Buzz. "They're just as good as Lefty and me."

"They'll have to do it," nodded Chip. "Say, Speed, you know what I think?" Without waiting for a reply he continued, "I think if we all worked with Lennie and Howie and went over all of Coach's stuff every night after practice, we'd be hard to beat. Lennie and Howie just don't know it well enough, that's all. Maybe we could all pitch in and teach it to 'em. What do you think?"

"Sounds good!" Speed assented. "We could move back everything here in the room and walk through the stuff. We'll have to—we play Delford in four days."

"That's time enough if you guys get together here every night and go over and over it," said Chip. He looked around the circle of faces. "Well, how about it?"

Bill English had been quiet all evening, but he voiced everyone's feelings when he said, "Look, the whole town's counting us out; everyone but the coach—he never quits! We won't quit either! Let's win those next two games if we have to practice all night!"

"That's the ticket!" Speed was on his feet and holding out his two hands. "What ya say, gang?"

Every boy in the room rushed to form the circle and join hands with his teammates. "We'll do it!"

The next morning Coach Rockwell was sitting stiffly behind his desk. His black eyes were focused steadily on Rogers' face.

"After all," Rogers was saying, "it's a police matter! You just can't do things like that when it's a police affair, Hank."

"We've got the money back! No harm's been done."

"It isn't a question of whether harm has been done, or not. You know that as well as I do. But the police have been investigating the matter for the past month. You'll never get away with it!"

"I'm not trying to get away with anything."

"Maybe not, but you're putting yourself in a position where you're sort of an accessory after the fact—have you thought about that?"

"Yes, I have."

"Okay, it's your funeral."

"There'll be no funeral. You know, Rogers, this might be just as good a time as any for you and me to get squared away." Coach Rockwell's voice was hard and his eyes had narrowed dangerously.

"You and I have been fencing about long enough. It's time you knew my philosophy about this teaching and coaching game. Teaching and coaching aren't just mediums for turning out mental wizards and athletic champions. They're something bigger. It's what you put into the heart and soul of a kid that counts. Not when he's on top and everything's okay, but when he needs help. Everyone's made mistakes; you made them, and I made them.

"Teaching and coaching gives fellows like you and me a chance to do more for a kid than his own father! Kids can *really* talk to us—and they do! And that's right where you and I differ; you don't feel that the teacher or the coach should get mixed up in a kid's personal or family problems—well, that's your business. I happen to feel the *other* way about it!

"Joel Ohlsen made a mistake. He needed help and I gave it to him—with *no* reservations. I told him I'd take care of his gambling checks and the money-box problem—*and I mean to do it!*

"Joel Ohlsen is the son of the most influential man in town; he could engineer your discharge and mine—but, as a father, well, as a father he's a good porter! You know it—and so do I! Joel Ohlsen has made a bad mistake, and he's got to be punished. But there are other ways to punish a kid besides throwing him in jail and putting a brand on him for life. That kid didn't have to tell me about taking that box—but he did! And what's more, he told his father too. We both know J. P. Ohlsen well enough to know he'll take care of the punishment end of it.

"I got my first insight into Joel Ohlsen's character when I had to throw him off the football squad. He showed me then what too much money and personal freedom can do to a boy's character. Joel probably has hated me ever since the football incident, too. But I'll bet you that Joel Ohlsen and I got closer together yesterday afternoon than he's *ever* been with his father.

"Most kids idealize and idolize anyone who's active

in sports. It's fellows like you and me—fellows who know the *real* score and who talk the kid's language—that the kid turns to when he's in trouble—

"Well, *I'm* not going to let that kid down! You handle the business end of the athletics; *I'll* handle the kids!"

CHAPTER 21

DOWN THE STRETCH

THE usual locker room banter and needling was missing. Old Pop and Chet looked at one another with puzzled eyes as they surveyed the grim, determined faces of the Big Reds. Little by little, the same spirit engulfed Chet and Pop; they worked quickly and quietly, strapping ankles and checking equipment.

Chip held his breath as he handed the scorebook to Rockwell. What if Rock didn't start Lennie and Howie! All their plans would go out the window!

He watched Rock pencil in the names: Morris, Schwartz, Browning— Rockwell hesitated and looked around the room. His eyes concentrated on the Scott twins for a second and then he quickly wrote down Scott and Scott.

Chip breathed a sigh of relief and caught Speed's eye. A grim smile passed between them—so far so good.

A slap on the back brought him about. Coach Rock-

173

well was regarding him with a quizzical smile. "Okay?"
he asked.

"I—I don't understand, Coach," Chip stammered.

"Isn't that what you've been holding secret practice
for—over at the Hilton A. C.?"

Chip was stumped for words. How did he do it? Jeeps
. . . he seemed to know everything. . . .

Coach Jenkins had his boys in a huddle in front of
their bench. Delford's center, Red Henry, towered
above the group. Jenkins was accentuating each word
as he struck the palm of his left hand with a clenched
right fist. "If you never win another game in your life,
win this one—let's knock them right out of the tournament! Tonight!"

The Delford-Valley Falls game always afforded bitter
competition, regardless of the quality of the teams. This
game was more like a grudge fight between Jenkins
and Rockwell. There was none of the usual handshak-
ing and friendly expressions of "good luck" before the
game—merely a cool "Hiya, Rock," and a "Hello,
Jenkins." And then the game was on.

Taps got a clean tap to Red Schwartz, and before the
game was ten seconds gone Valley Falls had scored on a
brilliant one-hand push shot by Speed. It was a fighting Big Red team that faced Delford. Delford didn't
have a chance—the first half was no contest. The Big
Reds were pouring it on with a vengeance. What a rebound! Howie and Lennie Scott were passing carefully
and playing the game just the way Coach Rockwell had
drilled Buzz Todd and Lefty Peters. Rockwell was

amazed at their cool play; they were never out of position in the backcourt, and their defense was perfect.

Speed and Red had discarded their famous give-and-go plays and were using Taps for a pivot blocking-post for play after play. Taps would maneuver under the basket until Speed and Red were all set—then he would break out and meet the ball. Speed and Red would "split the post" or drive their opponents into Taps for a block and then cut toward the basket for a return pass and a free shot.

Red Henry, the big Delford center, was good—but he had never been called upon to switch with every play. When Speed or Red cut by or in front of Taps, Henry had to switch or let them take an unguarded shot. Before the end of the second quarter he had four personal fouls charged against him. Speed and Red were too fast, and he had been forced to foul them as they drove in to the basket.

The fans had completely forgotten the upset by Dane; they cheered the Big Reds to the rafters. This was basketball as it should be played! At the half, Valley Falls led 31—20. The Big Reds had caught Delford unprepared. Coach Jenkins had scouted them thoroughly but was caught flat-footed. He had prepared a defense for the give-and-go specialties of Speed and Red and for Browning's under-the-basket shots but had mapped no defense for Coach Rockwell's new offense.

Between the halves the Valley Falls fans began to feel more the way they had after the triumphant road trip: "Rock is at it again!" "You can't keep the old boy down!" "You can see he's been working on those Scott kids—what a difference since the last game!" "Too bad they didn't play like that last week!"

But Coach Jenkins changed his defense for the second half. When Speed threw the first ball in to Taps, all five Delford players floated back between Taps and the basket. Gradually the gap closed: 31—22, 32—24, 32—26, 33—30; then Speed called time out.

Coach Rockwell was on his feet talking to Soapy Smith. Soapy was nodding his head and struggling out of his jacket. No longer did the other players nudge one another or make sly remarks when Soapy was sent into a game. The team had confidence in him now, and he had caught the fancy of the crowd. His never-say-die spirit and aggressive hustle had made him Coach Rockwell's first alternate for the starting five. Soapy had arrived!

Soapy dashed to the scorer's table, reported for Lennie Scott, and hurried into the huddle. There he began talking earnestly to Speed. When play was resumed, Speed and Red continued their cutting tactics, but now Taps was faking to them and then passing back to Soapy who took set shot after set shot at the basket. He was "hot," too, and within five minutes had scored ten points.

The Delford captain called time with the score, Valley Falls 43—Delford 33. The Delford second-half defense had been completely demoralized by the shift of Valley Falls' tactics; Soapy hadn't even been guarded when he took his shots at the basket. "Just like takin' candy from a baby," he was delightedly telling Speed and the gang in the huddle.

When play was resumed, Coach Rockwell's planned strategy repeatedly forced the Delford players into defensive errors. When they dropped back to stop Speed and Red, Taps passed out to Soapy on the side for a set shot; when they played Soapy close, Speed and Red cut under the basket and resumed their first-half attack. The game turned into a riot, and Coach Jenkins' bellowing could be heard all over the gym. The Rock was having a wonderful time! The final score: Valley Falls 54—Delford 38.

It wouldn't be long now! Next Friday night would tell the tale. Southern was scheduled to meet the Steelers at Steeltown and the tall Salem Sailors, in line for a tournament bid too, were the last team on the Big Reds' schedule.

What a race! Section Two hadn't seen anything like it in years. Three teams going into their last game of the season, each with thirteen victories and three defeats. Maybe there would have to be a play-off game. That was up to Southern's kids—

Speed dashed down the snow-covered steps as if he were on skis. Chip followed as best he could. The jalopy didn't even sputter when Speed stepped on the starter; nor did she groan when Chip, Taps, Soapy, and the Scott twins piled in with scrambling legs and arms. She was rarin' to go—and did. Sliding, screeching, banging, rattling, and running as hard as she could for the Hilton home and the radio. Yes, five minutes to make Stan Gomez and WTKO's eleven o'clock sportscast. No Sugar Bowl for Chip tonight!

Up on the porch, into the living room; over to the radio they raced. Speed turned the dial—

"Hello, sports fans. This is WTKO, Stan Gomez speaking, and bringing you sports headlines—right up to the minute. So, without further delay, let's turn to basketball and the state tournament.

"Weston—last year's state champion, as you know— finished the season with only two defeats—both by Valley Falls. The Cardinals, defending their great and unforgettable record of last year, were invited last Wednesday to participate in this year's tournament. Yes—and they're certain to be the top-seeded team—

"Here's a score that's hot off the griddle—hot from Steeltown where a major upset occurred tonight—"

"Yippee," yelled Soapy.

"They did it! They did it!" screeched Red. "Oh, boy—"

"Quiet," quavered Chip, "let's hear the rest of it."

"Yes—Southern defeated Steeltown tonight—yes— Southern. Final score: Southern 36—Steeltown 32. That was a heartbreaker for Steeltown. The Steelers were in a three-way tie with Salem and Valley Falls, you know. It was Steeltown's fourth defeat and ended their chances for the tournament—

"I'll have the dope on that Salem-Falls game in a minute now. Yes—that game Southern lost to Valley

Falls last week was the tip-off—the Big Reds were lucky to win that one—by a single point—

"And here's the score you've been waiting for—there was another upset tonight—"

"Here it comes!" exulted Soapy.

"Yes—the other upset occurred at Valley Falls. The Big Reds, playing their best basketball in weeks, upset the Salem Sailors 59 to 58. The Sailors had won thirteen out of sixteen—their last seven in a row—yep—the tallest team in the state met its match tonight when Soapy Smith, substitute star of the Big Reds, won his second game of the year by making good on a free throw in the last second of the game—"

"I'm a star! I'm a star!" Soapy was dancing a jig. "I'm a star!"

"Shut up or you'll see stars," threatened Speed with a happy grin.

"Smith broke a 58–58 deadlock with one second—one little second left to play. Yes—Soapy Smith not only broke that game wide open but broke the hearts of the Sailors as well—for that shot of Smith's put Valley Falls in undisputed possession of the runner-up position of Section Two—and the Big Reds right smack in the tournament—

"The state free-for-all starts next Friday afternoon at the University. Weston and Valley Falls finished Section Two, one-two and will represent their division for state honors. Each of the four sections send two representatives to the tourney, you know—"

"Can you imagine that—" began Soapy.

"Quiet a minute," Speed bellowed.

"—So now the tournament lines up with Weston and Valley Falls from Section Two—Waterbury from Section One—Rutledge and Seaburg from Section Four —and Bloomfield and Edgemont from Section Three. Yep—that's the way she lines up right now—only one place open—up in Section One. Looks as if Coreyville might get that berth. We'll know about that tomorrow night. And that, sports fans. . . ."

Speed snapped off the radio and fell back on the couch. "Boy, oh boy," he said. "Can you imagine those kids beating the Steelers?"

"Look out for Southern next year," said Lennie Scott.

Soapy's prophesy had come true; Valley Falls was in the tournament. One of the best eight teams in the whole state. In a few minutes they would be on their way—

Chip had been busy getting ready for the two-day stay at the university. Just a little while ago he had taken one last look at the trophy case and Valley Falls' first state championship ball—the one his dad had won. Maybe Speed and the gang could bring this year's ball back . . . maybe he could help bring one back next year. . . .

The bus which was to carry the team was purring in front of the gym steps. Standing around, talking, were just about everyone Chip could think of—Buzz Todd, Mike Sanders, Lefty Peters, Joe Kennedy, and Pete Williams—the papers were going to be well represented all right—Ted Williams, Biggie Cohen, and even Piggie Thomas.

Old Pop, dressed like a million dollars, nudged his way through the group. He waved a paper at Chip. "Here's the draw sheet, Chipper, right here in the paper."

They crowded around to look at the all-important pairings. Weston had been seeded number one, all right, just as Gomez had said. Waterbury had been seeded number two and had been paired with Valley Falls in the first round.

"We *would* draw them," someone said.

"We'll kill 'em!" said Soapy.

Pop passed the paper over to Chip, and each player studied the draw sheet carefully, mentally figuring the possible winners and the Big Reds' chances.

"Coreyville made it, didn't they," Taps remarked.

"Fill her in, Chip," urged Soapy. "Here, put Valley Falls right over there at the end—right there in the championship spot and then work back." He grabbed a pencil and leaned over Chip's shoulder to write "Valley Falls" on the championship line. "That's a pretty good draw sheet, now," he growled.

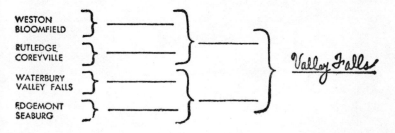

WESTON
BLOOMFIELD

RUTLEDGE
COREYVILLE

WATERBURY
VALLEY FALLS

EDGEMONT
SEABURG

Valley Falls

"Weston'll beat Bloomfield easy," said Speed.

"You're right," agreed Red. "Boy, wouldn't I like to meet them in the finals and beat 'em again!"

"Seaburg's a sleeper team, watch 'em," said Speed.

"Seems to me you guys better worry about Waterbury," laughed Chip.

CHAPTER 22

DARK HORSE
OF THE TOURNEY

CHIP used his player's badge to gain entrance to University gym and made his way through the usual corridor crowd toward the playing court. Just inside the tunnel leading to the playing court he paused in amazement—it was packed solid! He turned back and tried several other entrances with the same result; he couldn't even see the floor!

"How about that!" he muttered in disbelief. "Friday afternoon and standing room only!" What would happen tomorrow when the thousands of fans from all over the state began arriving for the Saturday afternoon and evening finals? He peered around desperately . . . this was no good . . . Rutledge was the team to beat . . . he had to see this game. . . .

Speed and he had been invited to University's spring athletic reception last year and they had worked-out on the court—that was it! Sure! He'd go down in the basement where the teams dressed and then come up on the playing court by the team entrance. . . .

Chip's hunch had been a good one. There were only a few officials and players standing in the team entrance and they were engrossed in the game. He edged a little closer to the long row of tables behind which were seated sports writers from every paper in the state. There was one vacant chair a little way along up the table. Before he realized it he was on his way to that chair. Sitting down, he drew out several sheets of the State Hotel stationery and began writing furiously. He felt as if all those twelve or fifteen thousand people were watching Chip Hilton . . . well . . . this was business. . . .

Right after lunch Coach Rockwell and Chet Stewart had put the players to bed. The tension and emotional pressure of an eight-team tournament in which the champion would be forced to win three games in two days made it imperative that every ounce of energy be conserved. After everyone was checked in, Chip had asked Coach Rockwell if he could watch the afternoon games.

Coach Rockwell smiled. "Sure, Chip," he said. "You might do a little scouting while you're at it, too. Rogers and Jerry Davis just left. S'pose you do a little scouting yourself, okay?"

Rutledge had been Chip's secret choice as the team to beat in the tournament. Burger was bigger than Weston's Fraling and had been burning up Section Four, scoring better than twenty points every game. He glanced at the scoreboard. Rutledge was leading Coreyville, 16—12. His glance shifted over to the other side of the court to the scorer's table . . . tonight *he* would be down there at that table and Speed and Taps and the gang would be out on the floor.

Scribbling as he watched, Chip wrote the notes on his program:

Rutledge uses a man-to-man defense . . . overshifts a little under the defensive basket . . . No. 14 is too slow . . . turns his head, too . . . Speed or Red could run him ragged . . . better put that down. . . .

Use quick break . . . good, too . . . after that, it's all Burger . . . knows what he's doin' all right . . . bigger'n Taps . . . stronger, too . . . long arms . . . seems a little slow . . . maybe Taps can outmaneuver him. . . .

Shoots rightie only . . . Coreyville's center isn't big enough to hold him . . . right-hand hook shot . . . better write that down several times . . . rightie only. . . .

"To beat Rutledge we have to do two things," Chip wrote. "One—stop their quick break; two—stop Burger!" He wrote that down several times. Taps could do it . . . Taps would *have* to do it. . . .

Coach Rockwell and Chet Stewart were seated in the lobby as Chip came hurrying in.

"All over?" queried Rockwell.

"Yes, sir! Weston and Rutledge! Rutledge looked awfully good, Coach!"

"Well, they're not in our bracket. We'll see how good they are when they meet Weston. We'll take them as they come, Chip."

"I've got some good notes on Rutledge, anyway, Coach."

"Looking pretty far ahead, aren't you?"

"Guess so, Coach, but I think they're the team to beat!"

The news-counter girl's smile changed to a blank look as Chip asked for a dollar's worth of *Morning Telegrams.* "A dollar's worth?"

"Yep, a dollar's worth!"

The girl glanced curiously at the big VF on Chip's sweater and then smiled again. "I get it," she said. "Did you win?"

"Sure did!"

"Going to win tonight?"

"Sure! That is, if we win this afternoon."

Chip noted that it was nine-fifteen by the lobby clock. The day's schedule called for a combination breakfast-lunch at eleven o'clock. That would be their only meal before the Seaburg game at two o'clock. Right after "brunch" a skull meeting was scheduled, to go over the Seaburg scouting notes and then a ten-minute walk and back to bed.

After the victory last night they'd had a terrific meal, fruit cocktail, soup, steak, roast potatoes, salad, and two big helpings of ice cream. Coach Rockwell had taken charge of the after-dinner walk and had given them a brisk fifteen-minute hike and then put them to bed with instructions to stay there until nine-thirty the next morning.

Chip went from room to room distributing the papers Coach Rockwell's dollar had bought, finally ending up in the room he shared with Taps. He threw Browning a paper and opened his own to the sports page.

WESTON ADVANCES TO QUARTER FINALS

RUTLEDGE, SEABURG, VALLEY FALLS ALSO WIN

The Weston Cardinals, last year's undefeated state champions defeated Bloomfield, Section-Three pace setter, in the opening game of the state tournament yesterday afternoon, 46—35. The Cardinals, led by their ace center, towering Perry Fraling, were in front all the way and played the last half under wraps.

Rutledge, seeded third, played possession basketball to win from a fighting Coreyville team by a score of 36—29.

In the first game last night Seaburg, runner-up to Rutledge in Section Four, easily disposed of Edgemont, champions of Section Three, 56—44.

In the final game of the first day's play Valley Falls created a mild sensation by upsetting Waterbury, Section-One leader, by a score of 47—42. Waterbury's two-three zone was riddled by the sharpshooting of Valley Falls' Morris and Schwartz.

Today's semifinals call for the Weston-Rutledge game at eleven o'clock this morning followed by the Seaburg-Valley Falls game at two o'clock this afternoon.

The third-place game will start promptly at seven o'clock tonight with the championship to be decided in the final game starting at eight-thirty sharp.

The Weston-Rutledge game this morning will pair up two of the best centers in the state; Perry Fraling, the Cardinal ace, will, for the first time this year, find himself up against a taller opponent. Larry Burger, Rutledge's one-man team, stands six feet seven inches and packs over two hundred pounds on his powerful frame. Weston rules a slight favorite in this game chiefly because of its tournament experience.

Seaburg is a strong favorite in the afternoon game. Rutledge nosed out the Sea Bees by the narrow margin of two points in the final game of Section Four's schedule. Valley Falls has a great star in Morris, and their upset victory over Waterbury stamps the Big Reds as the dark-horse team of this year's big show. However, it is doubtful if the Big Reds can match the height of the Sea Bees. Much depends upon Browning—

"I'll say it does," Chip muttered.

"What did you say?" Taps was nervous.

"Says here we're the dark horse of the tournament."

"That's good, isn't it? Anyhow we've got a chance to win third place."

"A chance to win *third* place! Are you kidding? What do you mean, third place? We didn't come up here to win third place—we came up here to win the *championship!*"

Anyone would have thought the squad of boys had been starved for a week. They tore into Coach Rockwell's "brunch" as if it were their last meal. You'd never have thought they had to play an important basketball game at two o'clock, either, by listening to the wisecracking and gales of laughter. But that was just what Coach Rockwell wanted—complete absence of pregame worry and tension.

Finally Rockwell and Chet Stewart came over to the table. "Okay, boys. Everyone feel all right? Good! A ten-minute walk, Chet. Then right back here to the sample room so we can go over those Seaburg notes."

Chip lingered behind, trying to catch Rockwell's eye. But it was wholly unnecessary—the coach beat him to the punch.

"Chip, you'd better rush over there and scout that Rutledge-Weston game. I've got a hunch your hunch is the right one—Rutledge!"

CHAPTER 23

LOCKER ROOM STRATEGY

CHIP heard the band before he saw it. The familiar strains of the Valley Falls Victory March greeted the bus as it turned up the drive and came to a stop in front of the main steps of the University gym. It was exactly 1:15. As they piled out they were nearly blown off their feet as the red-and-white-garbed band members ended the Victory March with a resounding blast. Principal Zimmerman had promised to send the band if the team won that first round. "We'll be there Saturday!" And they were!

Everyone was proud of the one hundred talented boys and girls who had won state honors more often even than the athletic teams. The Big Red school band was big time!

"Hiya, Speed." "Hello, Pop, how they feelin'?" "Hey! Soapy!" "What ya say, Red?" "Good luck, Rock!" "How about a ticket, Lennie?" "Knock 'em cold, gang!"

They were surrounded by about everyone they knew,

it seemed. Yep, practically everyone in Valley Falls had said that if the Big Reds won their first game they'd be there to see 'em win the championship!

Coach Rockwell and Chet led the determined squad through the pressing crowd of friends, up the steps, and to their dressing room. Even Soapy had no desire to trade jibes with some of his friendly hecklers. After the game they'd talk—now it was action!

Chip, holding the scorebook, leaned against the wall of the dressing room. Coach Rockwell was reviewing the Seaburg scouting notes.

"They're tall and they're good—but you're better! Use lots of bounce passes; keep the plane of your passing low—they'll intercept anything up in the air! But those tall kids don't like to bend over. Open 'em up! Don't jam up the center, Taps. I want you to move and keep moving! Ankle all right? Everyone feel okay? All right, then—go out there and win that game! Let's go!"

He held out his hand and everyone in the room rushed to join hands in that traditional sports circle which signifies team spirit and the bonding together for a common cause.

"Atta boy, Speed!" "Let's go, gang!"

They broke toward the door as if blown by a giant wind, pushing, elbowing, pounding one another, and shouting. Chip followed with Soapy's familiar "We'll kill 'em! We'll kill 'em!" ringing in his ears.

The crowd on the steps had been big, but this one was ten times as bad. The gap between the team and Chip

had closed, and he had no choice but to resign himself
to inch-by-inch progress. He was surrounded by shrieking boys and girls, laughing men and women, packed
like sardines. It seemed as if everyone had a hot dog
. . . everyone but himself . . . bantering, cheering,
pushing, laughing—

Up ahead there was a roar of applause, cheers, and
the thunder of a thousand Valley Falls fans as the Big
Reds dashed out on the floor. Chip finally got through
the big aisle. As he turned down the side of the court
toward the scorer's table, he saw the Big Red cheering
squad of eight boys and eight girls in formation in front
of the Valley Falls section. There was a brief quiet and
then the rafters shook—

> "Y - E - A—V - A - L - L - E - Y!
> Y-E-A—F-A-L-L-S!
> RAH!
> VALLEY FALLS!

Across the floor the Seaburg stands came right back
with a thundering cheer for the Sea Bees.

Chip looked up at the mezzanine and the two broad-
casting boxes. Draped below one was a big banner with
WTKO lettered upon it. Below the next box was the
WKMT banner. Stan Gomez and Smiley Harris were
on the job. He could see them peering down at the
crowd, and his thoughts leaped back to Valley Falls.
He could imagine the telephone office this afternoon—
bedlam! It would be worse tonight, he thought. Mom
probably would have to work overtime. . . .

Bet she'd have the little portable radio going, though.
. . . Guess 'bout everyone in Valley Falls was listening
in on Stan Gomez right now. . . .

Almost every town has a "Main Street." Main Street
in Valley Falls was a Saturday afternoon street. On any
other day it was fairly peaceful and quiet. But on Saturday afternoon you could meet nearly any one of Valley
Falls' twenty-five thousand citizens there at one hour or
another.

Not so today. It would have given you a strange feeling, if you knew Valley Falls, to see only a handful of
persons the whole length of the business section and to
hear the blaring of countless radios—all blending together with the reception of one broadcast, until it
seemed to fill every inch of space with a deafening roar.

"—Three minutes to go now—Seaburg leading by
seven points. There's a shot by Browning—he misses—
Browning looks tired—Sea Bees' ball now—they're coming down the court—taking their time—these boys play
a careful game—over to Billings—back to O'Brien—to
Warder—Seaburg's protecting that lead. There's a shot
by Billings—it's good! No—no—that's wrong—he
missed the basket—the light down at that north end is
bad—too dark with that crowd behind the basket—

"Morris has the ball—two minutes to play—he's up
to the ten-second line now—over to Schwartz—to Scott
—don't ask me which one—over to the other one—the
other Scott—he hooks the ball in to Browning—on the
free-throw line—that Seaburg defense is something to
see—Valley Falls can't get near the basket—

"Less than a minute to play now. Schwartz cuts by Browning and then drops back—Browning gives the redhead the ball—Schwartz shoots—it's good! Seaburg's lead is cut to five points now—time is running out —Seaburg is holding the ball—there's the gun!

"So—at the half, it's Seaburg 21, Valley Falls 16. And here's Randy White to review the first half of this semifinal game. Take it away, Randy—"

Ten seconds before the gun ended the first half, Coach Rockwell had cleared the bench. Chet Stewart had waited at the side of the court and had ushered Browning, Morris, Schwartz, and the Scott twins directly to the dressing room. Every one of those twelve intermission minutes was precious.

The Rock was talking:

"All right, pay attention now! That was a bad first half—I'm glad we've got *that* out of our system! You played right into their hands! They held the ball on the offense till they got a good shot—you drove in against their floating man-to-man defense and took bad shots!"

Coach Rockwell turned to the strategy board on the rubbing table and moved the five black chessmen back under one basket.

"How are you going to cut through a mob like that?" he demanded. "I waited for fifteen minutes before I saw a smart offensive play. What was the play, Speed?"

"Red's reverse offense play, Coach. Red passed to Taps, drove by him, and then fell back. Taps passed the ball back to Red and he got an easy set. Their whole team fell back when the ball went in to the post and Red cut toward the basket."

"Right! I talked about their floating defense until I was blue in the face when I went over the scouting notes; you can't cut through it. You've got to drive 'em back and then take those easy sets.

"On the defense you're letting them draw you out. You know their attack is all under the basket so why lunge and dive? Make them come to you. Understand?

"All right, so much for that! Now, *this* half, I want *you* to play possession ball, too. We'll give 'em a little of their own medicine. We're better passers, we're better shots, and our defense is just as good. I can't believe you're going to let Seaburg outsmart you.

"We'll keep driving in and driving 'em back and then we'll pass the ball out to Schwartz and Speed for sets. Then we'll follow in—Browning, Schwartz will follow in on every shot and tap or throw that ball back to Lennie—if we get it—and then we'll start all over again. Okay?

"We can take a chance on four men following in because they never quick-break—*never* quick-break, get that?

"On the defense, we'll stop lunging—we'll wait. We'll let them make the first move. Okay.

"Now, Lennie, you're in charge of the backcourt. You're the defensive quarterback. Don't get caught without help! Understand?

"Browning, Taps! You're the key to the attack. Don't try to dribble under the basket. Fake a shot, fake a pass, and then hook that ball back—hard—to Speed or Red. Understand?

"Now, Speed! I want you to take more time on your

sets. You're hurryin' your shots and you're not following through. There's no one near you; this is just like shootin' settin' ducks—like taking candy from a baby— if you do it right!

"And you, Schwartz. You start following through on your set shots, too. I want to see those hands finish up high. *High*, you understand?

"All right. This is it! Let's go!"

"—One minute to play. Seaburg leading by three points—they're freezing the ball—the Falls boys are pressing Seaburg all over the court—it's a dogfight down there—Warder has the ball now—Morris is playing him close—Warder dribbles to the coffin corner— he passes to Carroll—Schwartz is right on top of him— he may foul—thirty seconds now—the crowd is pushing out on the floor—this game is out of hand—twenty seconds—what a game! Billings has the ball—he's dribbling back along the side line toward the ten-second line—Morris is swarming all over him—ten seconds— There's a whistle—can't see what it's all about—looks like a foul on Morris—NO—it's Falls' ball out of bounds —Billings stepped on the side line—time is out!

"Morris is trying to get the ball—Billings won't give it up—the referee stopped the clock—Billings is still hanging onto the ball—he's lost his head—he throws the ball up in the crowd—the referee has called a technical—I think—yes—it's a technical foul—the ball is dead—eight seconds to go—Morris is on the line now— listen to that crowd—Morris shoots—it's GOOD!

"The referee is walking back to the middle of the court—it's going to be Falls' ball out of bounds at the ten-second line. There's eight seconds to play—this game isn't over yet, anything can happen. Morris is standing on the side lines—the referee hands him the ball—there's just eight little seconds to play—time isn't in until that ball crosses the side line—there it goes—Morris passes to Schwartz—back to Morris—in to Browning under the basket—he shoots—IT'S GOOD—IT'S GOOD!

"Folks, that's one for the book. Just as Browning pivoted and threw that ball toward the basket the gun ended the game—but the ball was in the air—the goal counts—the score's tied at 46 all now. There'll be a three-minute overtime period—wait a minute—

"There's something going on down there—the game's over but the referee's handing the ball to Browning on the free-throw line—Browning was fouled on the shot—he's to get a free throw—maybe there won't be that extra three-minute period after all—

"Browning is nervous—he bounces the ball on the floor—he's looking up at the basket—he shoots—IT'S ON THE RIM—IT'S IN! Valley Falls wins, 47 to 46!"

Back in Valley Falls a hysterical Petey Jackson was pounding John Schroeder on the back and shrieking at the top of his voice. The storeroom was crowded; had been since the start of the game. Anyone could have walked off with the cash register and half the store, and no one would have noticed it—or cared much!

"Shut up, you idiot," growled Doc Jones. "Listen!"

"—The Seaburg crowd is stunned, folks—they're swarming all over the floor—the scoreboard shows Valley Falls 47—Seaburg 46. The Falls crowd has Browning and Morris up on their shoulders—listen to those Big Red rooters!

"—This game will go down in state history, folks. You wouldn't believe it could happen—I still can't believe it. With eight seconds to go, Seaburg had the ball and a three-point lead—Seaburg would undoubtedly have won this game if Billings hadn't lost his head and delayed the game—that crowd pass of Billings' will be long remembered by the Seaburg fans—by the Valley Falls fans, too!"

CHAPTER 24

MOST VALUABLE
PLAYER

ONE point behind and fifty seconds to play. Rutledge was trying to freeze the ball. Burger would break out from beneath the basket and leap high in the air to get the ball. Taps was trying vainly to leap with him and tap the ball away but was missing each time.

Chip could almost read the thoughts passing through Taps' mind. He was trying to make up his mind whether to risk overrunning Burger in order to tap the ball away. If Taps overran Burger and the big Rutledge center caught the ball in spite of Taps' effort to strike it—he would be able to dribble in to his basket for an easy score and put the game on ice!

There wasn't much time left. Speed was playing "dummy," but this was a good team. They made few bad passes, and they kept the ball moving. Chip saw Taps gather his muscles. As Burger again drove out to the ball, Taps made a move to try for the interception, but his nerve failed him. He looked over to Chip. Their eyes met. Chip looked at the big clock—it was now or never! He rose to his feet and nodded his head with all his might. Taps nodded back.

Seconds later Burger broke out to the ball again. But this time Taps sped by him and leaped high in the air. His fingers barely touched the ball, but it was enough for Speed to dash in and make the catch. Chip looked at the clock—fifteen seconds to play!

Speed started a hard dribble for the basket but was blocked away. He turned, faked a shot at the basket, and then hesitated. Chip knew what Speed was thinking. Speed was figuring percentages. Even with the clock running out, Speed wouldn't lose his head . . . Speed wanted the best marksman on the floor to have that ball for the all-important shot. Soapy was standing over on the right side of the court, ready to follow in if Speed tried for the goal. Then Speed faked to Howie and threw the ball to Soapy.

"Take it, Soapy!" he yelled.

Soapy never hesitated. He let the ball fly straight for the basket. Chip, gripping the table for dear life, watched the flight of the ball. It was a little too hard . . . it might . . . yes . . . yes—but it didn't. The ball rebounded in the air on the left side of the basket. Speed had followed the shot and as the ball started its descent leaped high in the air with perfect timing and made the recovery. It seemed as though he was surrounded by the entire Rutledge team, but he managed somehow to turn and twist in the air and throw the ball right back to Soapy. Chip's mind flew back to Sy Barrett's famous shot. . . .

Soapy had hardly moved from his position. When the ball came flying back to him he stood as if powerless to move.

"Shoot!" "Stop him!" "Shoot!" "Stop him!"

Soapy's opponent had turned away from him and followed the ball toward the basket for the rebound. Soapy was wholly unguarded. Chip's frantic eyes darted to the clock—"two seconds!"

"Shoot!"

Then Soapy leaped with the shot and, as the ball arched high in the air, the timer's gun exploded. The ball was spinning toward the basket and every person in the gym was on his feet, eyes glued to the flying sphere. Not a player on the floor moved as the ball swished through the net to make Valley Falls STATE CHAMPIONS!

Chip dropped back in his chair. He didn't even mark the score in the book. He sat with his eyes glued on the scoreboard: Valley Falls 54—Rutledge 53.

Forever and ever, people in Valley Falls would talk about Soapy's shot; just as they had talked about Sy Barrett's. What a guy, that Soapy. . . .

Speed grabbed the ball out of the hands of the protesting referee and ran over to help the gang get Coach Rockwell on their shoulders. The Valley Falls rooters had already elevated Soapy and now he was gaily making a speech:

"It was this way—"

They carried Rockwell and Soapy out to the center of the court where the big trophy was to be presented.

Chip was holding his precious scorebook as if it were made of solid gold. When the cup was presented, the gang let Coach Rockwell scramble down but kept Soapy up in the air. Soapy liked it! He was throwing kisses, patting himself on the chest, and talking a mile a minute. "You see, it was like this—"

When they posed for the photographers, Coach Rockwell put his arm around Chip's shoulder, and Speed gripped him by the arm on the other side. Behind him a towering Taps was rumpling his hair and shouting something—Chip had never been so happy in his whole life. . . .

As soon as the pictures were finished, they started through the crowd for their dressing room. Chip held the scorebook high and kept shouting the score, "Fifty-four to fifty-three! fifty-four to fifty-three!"

Coach Rockwell was holding the big trophy—STATE CHAMPS!

Across the floor they barged, digging elbows, pushing shoulders, yelling hilariously. Speed was fighting his way through the crowd, his right hand pushing people aside while he clutched the championship ball under his left arm. Chip was carried along with the crowd and just managed to squeeze inside the dressing room.

It was a madhouse! Everyone was shouting, yelling, throwing towels, shoes, sweat coats, everything and anything they could get their hands on. Outside, the hall was filled with a throng of cheering friends and fans.

This was one night that Coach Rockwell's "no visitors" rule was forgotten. Most of Chip's crowd was there, yelling and having the time of their lives. Here and there were a few photographers and newspaper writers trying to get a word in edgewise or take a picture but having no success. Cheering friends and happy parents; pushing, slapping backs; wildly celebrating.

Coach Rockwell was standing on the rubbing table in the center of the room trying to get the team's attention. "Boys—" He paused and looked around. "Boys," he said when they had quieted, "we've got to make an important decision tonight—now!" He held the championship ball up in the air.

"This is Valley Falls' first state championship ball in eight long years. You know the tradition—the championship ball is always given to the fellow who does the most to win it. We've got to decide who gets this ball. Here, Chet, mark down the votes. Who gets the—"

The sentence was never finished for a roar went up from Chip's teammates which drowned out everything else: "Hilton! Chip! Chip Hilton!"

"GIVE IT TO CHIP!"

Chip heard the shout as from far off—but it didn't register. Then he knew that Speed was pushing him up on the table and Coach Rockwell was slapping him on the back of the head easylike, and smiling—and he was holding the championship ball. . . .

He tried to speak, but there just wasn't any room in his throat for words to get past the something which seemed as big as a basketball and which had lodged halfway between his heart and his mouth; it was surely going to suffocate him . . . what was this all about. . . .

Slowly it sank in . . . this was no dream. . . . The gang and Coach were giving *him* the championship ball! Why? Why he wasn't even on the team! *This* wasn't right! He tried to push the ball back, but Coach Rockwell's hands were like steel bands on his arms—holding him helpless.

As the wild cheering quieted, Coach Rockwell shook him gently and said, "Hilton, you worked harder than all of us put together to win this ball. There wouldn't have been a championship ball if it hadn't been for your spirit and devotion to the team. A championship ball for a real champion!"

There was a scramble of legs and arms and Speed was up on the table beside him. "How's about a cheer?" he yelled. "Come on, gang, let's go!"

"Y-e-a H-i-l-t-o-n! YEA CHIP! CHIP HILTON!"

CHAPTER 25

HIS FATHER'S SON

SLEEP was impossible. Chip had been awake long before his mother began stirring around in the kitchen. He joined her at the breakfast table and they discussed the celebration of the evening before; the bonfire on the square and the snake dance down Main Street.

Later, pasting the tournament clippings in his scrapbook, Chip's thoughts traveled back to that day he had argued with Speed . . . the day he had lost his head and thrown the book across the room. . . . Those pages of clippings meant something after all. . . .

The ring of the doorbell jarred him back to the present and he went out into the hall. It was Doc Jones.

"Hiya, Chip. I thought I'd drop over and shake your hand! Couldn't get near you last night at the celebration. Just wanted to congratulate you for winning the ball!"

"Gee, Doc—I don't feel right about that ball. I'm

awfully proud of it, of course, but—well, I just don't deserve it."

"No?" Doc Jones shook a finger under Chip's nose. "Well, boy, let me tell you something about youngsters you don't know. Kids don't spread any molasses where their hearts are concerned. They gave you that ball because they honestly believed you were entitled to it and, knowing all the things I do about your work with that team, they were absolutely right!"

"Yes, but—"

"No buts! By the way, how's your leg?"

"Why, fine, Doc—I guess. I never think much about it now, seems like."

"Got your brace on now?"

"Yes, sir—sure, Doc."

"Well, s'pose we go in the living room and take it off. I'd like to take a look at that ankle—"

In the living room the conversation shifted back to basketball. Finally, Doc Jones stood up, shifting the brace from one hand to the other. "Well, I've got to go, Chipper. Drop up to the office sometime."

Chip followed him to the porch. Good old Doc. . . .

"You forgot the brace, Doc."

"Oh, so I did, so I did. It's been a pretty good one, hasn't it?"

"Sure has, Doc."

"Well, so long again, Chip." He started down the steps.

"But the brace, Doc"

"Oh—oh, yes. Well, I'll give it to someone who needs it, Chip."

"Someone who *needs*—Doc! Doc—don't I—don't I need it?"

"You?" Doc Jones laughed. "I don't see what for."

"You mean I can walk without it, Doc?"

"Did pretty well just now!"

"And I can go upstairs without it?"

"Sure! If you want to!"

"You mean, Doc, I can maybe *run* without it—"

"You used to be pretty fast!"

"And—and—can I play baseball?"

"You always could!"

"You *really* mean it, Doc?"

"Did I ever fool you, Chipper?"

"Holey socks! So long!"

At the foot of the stairs he stopped. He was bewildered. He turned and dashed into the living room and grabbed the championship ball from the table, muttering to himself a mile a minute, "And when it goes, he'll never know—EE-YI, EE-YI, OH!"

A thousand thoughts rushed madly through his mind. "I'll take the ball over to the gym . . . Coach said he's gonna put it in the trophy case alongside Dad's! Hope he's there . . . just gotta tell him the news . . . gotta tell everybody. . . . I'll call Mom. . . . EE-YI, EE-YI, OH!"

He hurried toward the school. As he turned the corner, he saw Coach Rockwell slowly ascending the steps to the gym. Quickening his pace he darted forward and, without thinking, dashed up the steps.

Rockwell heard him coming and stopped at the landing.

"Why, Chip! How about your leg?"

"I can run, Coach! I don't have to wear my brace any more! See? It's gone! I—I—I can even play baseball! Doc says it's as good as new—"

Chip looked up at the remaining steps . . . twenty-five . . . twenty-six . . . twenty-seven . . . twenty-eight . . . twenty-nine . . . thirty. . . .

"Look, Coach!" With a mighty spring he took the short flight three at a time.

Standing in front of the trophy case Chip gazed at two championship balls—side by side. He remembered Coach Rockwell's words: "If your dad were in your shoes he'd be right in there pitching, giving all he had for the team, whether he was the star, a sub on the bench, or the manager!"

All the worries and all the events of the past months came flooding back to him. Now it was all as clear as a picture. . . . He could see and understand it all. . . .

Why, Speed, Taps, and Coach had planned all along to make him manager. . . . From the very beginning Speed had needled him into fighting back, and Taps had put on an act for days on end with the pivot stuff. . . .

Now, he reflected, he could understand why Taps

looked so bad when he was practicing with him . . .
and then looked so marvelous in the games. . . . Hood-
winked all the way. . . .

Chip wished he could put into words all the things
he wanted so desperately to say to Coach and Speed
and Taps and all the gang . . . what they had meant
to him. . . . What the ball had meant, too. . . .

And the steps . . . yes . . . those thousands of steps
he had counted during the past four months. . . . Why
to earn that ball he would have crawled up every one
of those steps . . . one by one . . . a million times!
Nothing would ever have been important in his life if
he hadn't whipped his crybaby stuff—if he couldn't
have been near the gang—and the Rock. . . .

Chip turned away from the trophy case to speak to
Coach Rockwell, but he had disappeared. A wave of
gratitude swept over the boy as he stood there alone in
the gym foyer, and a mist came over his eyes and a
painful lump gathered in his throat. Suddenly he
realized that the months that had passed since that dis-
heartening day when he had come home from the
hospital would always remain the most important in
his life.

Slowly, but with no sign of a limp, he walked over to
one of the windows through which the March sun was
streaming. It was one of those balmy days in late winter
when spring seemed to be just around the corner despite the piles of dirty snow that lined the sidewalks.
From across the street came a rhythmic thump, a sound

produced only by a baseball thudding into a catcher's mitt. Two kids were playing catch in the driveway across the street. Chip executed an imaginary speedy tag on a runner sliding home and charged for the door and the flight of steps that led to the sidewalk.

Your Score Card—
of CLAIR BEE'S Famous
CHIP HILTON SPORTS STORIES

I have read: *I expect to read:*

☐ ☐ **(1) TOUCHDOWN PASS** The first story in the series which introduces you to Chip Hilton and all his pals at Valley Falls High. A corking football story in the bargain.

☐ ☐ **(2) CHAMPIONSHIP BALL** With one bum leg and an unquenchable spirit Chip wins the state basketball championship and an even greater victory over himself.

☐ ☐ **(3) STRIKE THREE** In the hour of his team's greatest need Chip Hilton takes the pitcher's box and puts the Big Reds in line for the all-state honors.

☐ ☐ **(4) CLUTCH HITTER** Chip Hilton plays summer ball on the famous "Steeler" team and has a chance to use his head as well as his war-club.

☐ ☐ **(5) HOOP CRAZY** When the one-hand-shooting fever spreads to the Valley Falls basketball varsity, Chip Hilton has to do something, and do it fast!

☐ ☐ **(6) PITCHERS' DUEL** Valley Falls participates in the State Baseball Tournament and Chip Hilton pitches in a nineteen inning struggle that fans will long remember.

☐ ☐ **(7) A PASS AND A PRAYER** Chip's last football game for the Big Reds and how he kept the team together for his old coach.

☐ ☐ **(8) DUGOUT JINX** The story of the summer Chip spent with a professional team during its battle for the league pennant.

☐ ☐ **(9) FRESHMAN QUARTERBACK** This story finds Chip and some of his pals up at the State U. where the young star finds it tough to win a spot on the Frosh team.

Your local Bookseller has all of these books!

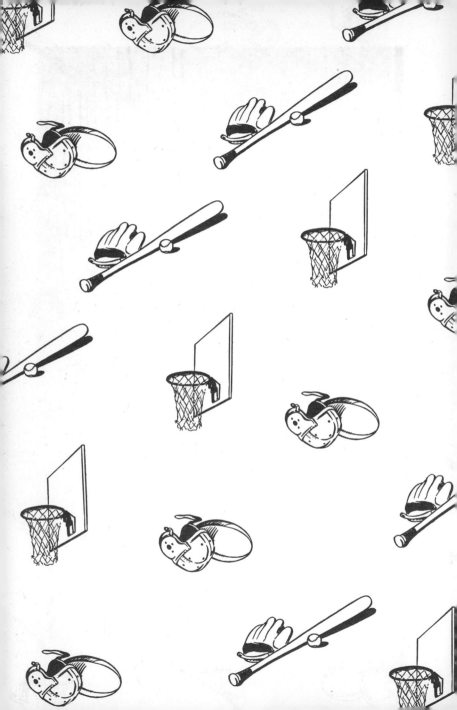